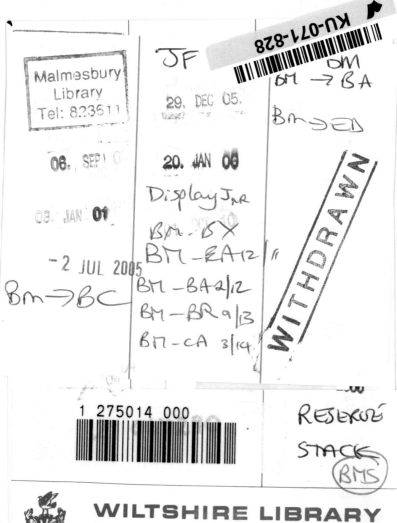

WILTSHIRE LIBRARY & MUSEUM SERVICE

Headquarters : Bythesea Road, Trowbridge.

Items should be returned to the library from which they were borrowed on or before the date stamped above, unless a renewal has been granted.

GRIMM'S FAIRY TALES

GRIMM'S FAIRY TALES

RETOLD BY AMABEL WILLIAMS-ELLIS

ILLUSTRATED BY FRITZ WEGNER

BLACKIE: GLASGOW AND LONDON

ISBN 0 216 90468 4

Blackie & Son Limited
Bishopbriggs, Glasgow G64 2NZ
450/452 Edgware Road, London W2 1EG

Printed in Great Britain by
Robert MacLehose and Company Limited
Printers to the University of Glasgow

Contents

— ❦ —

TO
JULIAN, JESSICA, MARTIN,
RACHEL AND CATHERINE
WITH MUCH LOVE

SNOW-WHITE AND ROSE-RED

A POOR WIDOW ONCE LIVED WITH HER TWO daughters in a lonely cottage at the edge of a forest. The cottage was pretty and neat and in the garden, one on each side of the path, grew two rose trees. All the summer long one would be covered with white roses and the other with red. Perhaps it was because of these flowers that her two little girls were always called Snow-White and Rose-Red.

Snow-White was very fair, with blue eyes and long silky hair, while Rose-Red had dark curling hair, sparkling black eyes and rosy cheeks. The two children were very fond of each other and generally went about together.

Their mother was glad to have two such good and friendly children and, as long as they were together, she never feared that any harm would come to them. So they often went into the fields and the forest alone, either just for a walk or to pick flowers in the summer or berries or mushrooms in the autumn. Sometimes their mother would send them to collect a sack of firewood, or down to the stream to try to catch some fish for dinner. They were quite used to all the animals that lived in the forest: and it really seemed as though not even the fiercest creatures would do the pretty little sisters any harm. In fine weather, in the summer, they would sometimes even spend the night in the forest, curled up together on the soft moss that grew under the trees, and wouldn't go home till it was light again. Their mother was sure that as long as they were together they were quite safe, so she never either worried or scolded them if they did this.

In the winter it was different and the two little girls always stayed at home after dark. The winters are very cold in those parts, snow covered the ground for months, and their fun in the frosty time when the nights were long was to polish up the copper cooking-pans and the furniture till everything shone. After supper it would generally turn bitterly cold outside. But when the door was shut and bolted and when the firelight winked and blinked cosily in the warm kitchen and shone reflected in their polished pans, everything indoors looked cheerful. Their mother would often light a candle and the two girls would get out their spindles and, as they sat by the warm fireside, they would spin while she read to them out of a big book.

One evening when the frost was hard, as they were sitting like this, there came a loud knocking at the door.

"Open the door, Rose-Red," said the mother, "that must be some poor traveller who has lost his way. Be quick, he must be half frozen, it's bitter cold outside!"

Rose-Red jumped up, pushed back the big bolt and began to open the door. But all of a sudden she screamed, for instead of a lost, shivering traveller, what should she see but a very large shaggy black bear! He peered round the door blinking in the light, and when Snow-White, too, caught sight of his broad black head, both the children were so frightened that they ran and hid behind their mother's bed. But now the bear began to speak in a deep hoarse voice.

"Don't be afraid!" he said. "Only let me come in and warm myself a little! I'm half frozen! I'll do you no harm!"

"Poor bear!" said the mother, putting down her spectacles. "Come in and lie down by the fire! Only mind you don't get too close and singe your fur."

So the huge shaggy creature pushed the door wide and came in and lay down, peaceably enough, while the mother got up and shut the door after him to keep out the cold.

"Snow-White! Rose-Red!" called she. "Come out! The bear is quite friendly!"

So the two little girls came out and stood looking rather doubtfully at the huge black creature.

"Children," said the bear in his deep growling voice, "could you please knock some of the snow out of my coat?"

Rather timidly they fetched the big house-brush and began to sweep the melting snow out of the bear's thick, heavy fur. It was like sweeping a very thick carpet! As they brushed, the bear kept turning and stretching himself, this way and that, as if he enjoyed it. Soon he seemed to be quite warm and dry again and began grunting contentedly, for all the world as if he were a great purring cat.

Now these two girls were used to animals, and though they had been so much frightened at first, this brushing and sweeping soon made them feel quite at home with the big, sleepy, clumsy creature, so that it wasn't long before they began to pound him with their fists and tug at his fur under pretence of getting more snow off, and at last they were climbing all over him as he lay. They got so rough that they almost knocked the breath out of the bear

11

so that he grunted aloud, and then the two children laughed.

The bear took all this play in good part, and only said, now and then, "Leave me alive, children. Don't kill me!"

> "Snowy-White and Rosy-Red,
> Will you beat your lover dead?"

At last, when it got late and she had sent the children to bed, the mother banked up the fire with ashes, put out the candle, said goodnight to the bear, and, as she too went to bed, she told him that he might lie by the warm hearth till morning.

As soon as daylight came he seemed anxious to be off, so the children opened the door, and watched him trot across the snow and disappear into the forest.

And now, all that winter, every evening, the bear came at the same time, exactly as he had done on the first night. He knocked at the door, the children opened it for him, and he lay down on the hearth directly and let the children brush out the snow and play with him till he could bear it no longer and had to beg for mercy.

> "Snowy-White and Rosy-Red,
> Will you beat your lover dead?"

After a while, they all got so used to him that the door was never bolted till their large black friend had arrived.

— 2 —

At last, when spring came, and when the sun shone warm once more, and the soaked meadows grew green again, the bear said to Snow-White one morning:

"Now I must go away, and not come back for the whole summer."

"Where are you going, dear bear?" asked she.

"I must stay in the forest to look after my treasure," said he. "Some dwarfs are good, but the dwarfs that live round here are as spiteful as can be, and they're a pack of thieves into the bargain."

"Don't they steal in the winter?" asked Snow-White.

"No," said the bear. "Treasure is safe from them as long as the ground is frozen hard. They go below before it freezes to keep warm, and there they have to stay. They can't work their way through the hard ground, but as soon as the earth has thawed soft again, out they come, the spiteful thieving creatures! These dwarfs will always do a bad turn if they can. They steal anything valuable that they can lay their hands on, and once they've managed to carry a thing down into their caves, it doesn't often see daylight again."

Snow-White felt sorry to think that they wouldn't see their black friend for such a long time. However, as he seemed determined to go, she unbolted the door for him. As he was hurrying out he caught his fur on the latch and tore out a bit of his shaggy coat. It seemed to Snow-White as if, as he did it, she had seen something glittering like gold under the black fur, but she wasn't sure about it, for the bear was in such a hurry that he didn't turn to wait, but trotted off directly and was soon out of sight among the trees.

Now, they had of course had good fires all winter, so, by this time, the store of firewood which they kept dry under the broad eaves of the cottage had nearly all been used up. As the weather was fine, their mother sent the two children out into the forest to get some more.

They hadn't gone far when, in the distance, they saw a big tree lying on the ground, and thought they would be able to chop off some of the smaller branches. As they got nearer they saw that, close by the trunk, something small seemed to be jumping backwards and forwards on the grass. But it wasn't till they got quite close that they saw that this something wasn't a squirrel or a mouse but a little dwarf. He had a white beard as long as himself, and a bad-tempered, withered face, and they could see that what had happened was that his beard had somehow got caught in the tree. The angry little creature was jumping backwards and forwards like a chained-up dog, and, as they got nearer, he glared at them out of his two red eyes.

"What are you two standing there for?" he called out in a cross, squeaky voice. "Come and help me, you stupid creatures!"

"What's the matter, little man?" asked Rose-Red.

"What's that to you, you inquisitive thing?" answered he. The children said nothing, so he went on sulkily, "If you must know, I was trying to split a little bit from this tree for some wood for cooking. Big logs are no good, they get too hot! The little bit of food that one of us wants gets burnt up directly with thick logs! I'd just driven my wedge in nicely when out the wretched thing flew again and now the split has closed on my beautiful white beard! Can't you see?"

"I'm so sorry!" said Snow-White kindly, but neither of the girls could help smiling a little, because the cross little creature looked so funny.

"Don't stand there grinning and saying you're sorry, you silly milk-faced things!" screamed the dwarf. "Do something to help, and be quick about it!"

"Don't be so impatient, little man," said Snow-White. "I'll help you," and with that she pulled her scissors out of her pocket, and cut off just the tip of his long white beard.

14

No sooner did the dwarf feel himself free than he stooped down, and snatched up a bag of gold which lay at the roots of the tree. He lifted it on to his back without a word of thanks and all the time grumbling to himself:

"Fancy cutting off a piece of my fine beard! Wretched creatures!" Then, off he went, and indeed the last thing he did was to call down bad luck on the children who had helped him.

Quite a long time after that their mother sent Snow-White and Rose-Red down to the stream to see if they could catch some fish for dinner. As they came near the water they could see that something was jumping and hopping along by the stream and that with each hop it seemed to be getting closer to the water. It looked as if a large grasshopper was just going to jump into the little river. Running forward to see what this could possibly be, they saw that it was the dwarf again.

"Where are you going?" called out Rose-Red. "You'll be in the water in a minute if you go on like that!"

"Don't you see, you stupid creature?" screamed the dwarf. "It's this wretched fish that's trying to pull me in!"

What had happened was that the little man had been sitting there fishing. The wind had happened to catch his beard and had tangled it up with the fishing-line, just at the moment when a big fish had taken the hook. The fish had pulled and the dwarf had pulled, but now—by the time the girls saw him—the fish had begun to get the better of it, and, though the dwarf held on to all the clumps of reed and rushes as he passed, in another minute he would have been pulled, splash! into the water. The two girls lost no time. One held the dwarf fast and the other tried to untwist his beard from the line. But it was all in vain for the fish kept jumping and pulling so much that try as they would, the tangle only got worse. There was nothing to be done but to bring out the scissors again and once more to cut his beard.

This time the dwarf was absolutely furious and his voice rose to a regular squeak.

"You toadstool!" he cried to Rose-Red. "What a mess you've made of my face between you! First one of you cuts off the tip, and now, today, the other one has cut off the best part of my beautiful beard! I shan't dare to show myself to the other dwarfs!" And with that, trembling with rage, he picked up another sack—full of pearls this one was—which had been hidden in the rushes. Then he hoisted the sack on to his back, and once more without a word or even a look of thanks, he disappeared among the willows.

Quite a long time passed, but the two girls didn't see the dwarf again. Then, one day in the autumn, their mother sent them to the town, to buy needles and thread and a few other things she needed for sewing their winter dresses. They were nearly grown up now so that their little girls' dresses were no good to them.

The way to the town lay across a big bare heath where heather and bog-myrtle grew and where huge pieces of rock lay strewn here and there. As they walked along, the girls noticed a huge bird which hovered in the air or sailed slowly round and round on its outspread wings, sometimes almost above them. At last they saw the eagle dart off and then swoop down behind a rock which was not far off. As soon as it dropped they heard a loud and pitiful screaming, and running up they saw that the huge bird was seizing their old acquaintance, the dwarf, in its talons. It was plain that the eagle was just going to

16

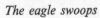

The eagle swoops

make off with him. Full of pity, the girls reached up and took hold of the little man and, pulling and tugging, they managed to get him out of the eagle's claws and to drive off the great bird.

17

For a moment the frightened dwarf lay on the ground, not saying anything. Then at last he sat up, looked himself over, and then shouted in his shrill voice:

"Couldn't you have done it more carefully? You've dragged at my brown coat so that it's all torn! Look, it's full of holes! Clumsy creatures!" Then he got to his feet and again picked up a bag—full of all sorts of precious stones this time—and, once more without a word or a look to say Thank you, he slipped away among the rocks.

The two girls, who were, by this time, quite used to the dwarf's bad temper and rude ways, only laughed a little and went on their way to the town and thought no more of what had happened.

On the way home, when they had done their shopping and as they crossed the heath again, they decided to take a short cut, and there, near a flat piece of rock, they saw the dwarf. He had laid out all the precious stones that had been in his bag, on the flat rock, never thinking that anyone would come along so late. The evening sun shone on the bright jewels, which glistened and sparkled, green, blue and fiery red, while the diamonds flashed white. They looked so beautiful that the two girls stood still for a moment to look at them.

"Why do you stand there gaping?" cried the dwarf. "What are you doing here? Spying on me, I suppose!" His ash-grey face went copper-red with rage as he spoke and he began to shake his little fist at them. "Be off with you!"

Just as he finished screaming at them there was a sound like a deep growl, and what should come trotting round one of the rocks, but a large black bear. The dwarf who had been so bold and rude to the girls took fright at once, when he saw the bear, but he had no time to run, still less to gather up the rubies, emeralds, sapphires and diamonds, for the great animal was quite close.

"Dear Mr. Bear, spare me!" begged the dwarf, dropping to his knees and speaking in a voice that trembled with fright. "You can have all my treasure! You can have all these precious stones. Don't eat me! Eat these two great girls instead! They'll make you a lovely dinner! They're as fat as young quails. For mercy's sake, eat them!"

The bear, who had stood quite still while the dwarf was speaking, now gave another deep growl, reared up on his hind legs, then, with a heavy front paw, he gave the wicked little creature one blow. The blow would have killed a much heavier creature than the dwarf, who now lay there dead, sprawled across his stolen jewels.

While all this was going on and while the ungrateful dwarf was inviting the bear to eat them, the two girls had run off in a fright, but as they ran, they soon heard a familiar voice calling to them:

"Snow-White! Rose-Red! Don't be afraid! Wait for me!"

They then knew that the bear was none other than their old friend who had so often warmed himself at their fire and so, no longer afraid, but very much pleased, they waited for him. When he came up with them, great was their surprise when suddenly the rough bearskin fell off him, and before them there stood a handsome young man, all dressed in crimson and gold.

"I am a king's son," he said, "and I was bewitched by that wicked dwarf who had also stolen all my treasure. But now at last the spell is broken, and the dwarf has got the punishment he deserved."

So they all three started off home to the cottage to tell

the girl's mother what had happened and a merry evening they all had when she had heard the tale.

Next day the Prince had to go back to his father, the King, but before he went he promised to come back in a year and a day.

Faithful to his word he did come back and not only did he come himself, but he brought with him his younger brother. The end of it was that he asked Snow-White to marry him, and Rose-Red was asked in marriage by his brother.

As soon as they were married they all four went in search of the stolen treasure which they felt sure the dwarf must have gathered together in his cave.

When they had found it, and when it was time for Snow-White and Rose-Red to go back with them to their father's kingdom, their old mother came too and with her she took the two rose trees that had stood for so long on either side of the path of the cottage.

She planted them again, one on each side of her window, and she watered them carefully. And now once more, every summer, for many years, they were both covered, thick, with beautiful roses—snow-white and rose-red.

MRS. OWL

THREE OR FOUR HUNDRED YEARS AGO THERE WAS a little town in Germany where the people weren't as clever as people are nowadays, and something happened in that very town that filled the townsfolk with such terror that they talked of it for years afterwards. This was how it all began.

One night, not long before dawn, a large owl—one of the sort with two tufts of feathers that look rather like horns—happened to fly softly on her silent wings into a certain barn that belonged to one of the townspeople. Soon the owl, as she hunted about for mice, noticed that, outside, it was beginning to get quite light. She didn't like daylight so she thought she had better stay where she was in the nice dark barn and spend the day hiding. It wasn't so much the light that she minded but—as you know—when owls come out in daylight, sparrows and all the other little birds like to come and mob them. They can't hurt them really but they fly round them chirruping and abusing them, till even a big owl feels quite flustered. So this owl, who was rather easily put out, decided to perch on a comfortable beam, and to stay in the twilight barn, till—once again—it got nice and dark and safe for her outside.

Soon the sun rose and the townspeople began to wake up, and a manservant came whistling out to the barn to fetch some straw. What should he see when he opened the barn door, but Mrs. Owl's two great gleaming eyes in the light that came through the open door. He was so terrified at the sight that he rushed out again in a fright, shutting the door behind him.

"Master, master!" cried he. "There's a huge monster in the barn the like of which I never saw before! It stared at me with its great eyes! It must be huge for its eyes were right up above my head!"

"Don't be such a coward," said his master. "I know you! You are hardly brave enough to chase a blackbird! You're the sort that has to get a stick before you dare go near a dead hen! I'm sure there can't be a monster in our barn." So the master, angrily pushing the servant aside, went to his barn to see for himself. But no sooner had he opened the door than he saw Mrs. Owl's eyes gleaming in the light. He was just as much frightened at the sight as his servant had been and, shutting the door behind him, he ran as fast as he could to fetch the neighbours.

"Help! Help! Come quickly, neighbours!" cried he. "There's a terrible beast in my barn. I've shut it up, but the whole town would be in danger if it were to break loose! Come and help!"

So a whole crowd of his neighbours came, all armed with hay-forks, scythes and axes.

The mayor soon heard the commotion, and he told the town council that something terrible must be going on. So putting on their robes, he and the aldermen and councillors all joined in, and it wasn't long before the mayor had got all the townsfolk drawn up in the square just as if they had been a regular army. Then he gave his orders and marched them all down to the barn.

"Left, Right! Left, Right!" "Right Turn! Left Turn! Halt!" And so, like that, they got the barn properly surrounded.

But now someone had to be found who would dare to open one of the big barn doors. At last the bravest of the aldermen, one who had got a real spear, opened one door and waving farewell to the rest of the town council he took a step inside the barn. But he rushed out again in a moment, pale as death, and so frightened that he could not utter a word to tell the others what he had seen. Two others tried it, but they fared no better. So a council of war of all the townsfolk was held. At last a big strong man spoke up. He had always told splendid tales of his warlike deeds, so, when he spoke, everyone in the crowd listened.

"The mayor and the councillors can't manage a job like this!" said he. "They can't drive away the monster by just looking. I will see what I can do! Get me some armour, a spear and a sword!" At that the crowd began to cheer and everyone praised the strong man's courage. But the women said it was a shame that such a gallant fellow, a man in the prime of life too, should take such a terrible risk! At last, however, the brave champion was dressed in armour from head to foot, and then not one, but both the great doors of the barn were flung open.

In the meantime Mrs. Owl, disturbed by so much coming and going, had perched herself on what she thought was a safer beam, so that now her big glowing eyes shone down from even higher. The champion could not reach her.

"Bring me a ladder!" cried he. "For in the name of St. George who slew the dragon, I will surely rid the town of this terrible monster!"

Up the ladder he went clanking, and when she saw him coming closer, Mrs. Owl, worried by so much light and all the shouting—and now by all this clatter of armour—began to flap her wings and roll her eyes and even to snap at him with her beak.

"Strike home! Strike home!" cried the crowd.

"Tu whit tu whoo!" cried Mrs. Owl.

Mrs. Owl terrifies the champion

But, at that dreadful sound of "Tu whit tu whoo", with a clang of armour, the valiant champion fell fainting off the ladder; it took four brave men to carry him out.

"Shut the doors! Shut the doors!" shouted the crowd when he was safe outside. Those who had been able to see, told terrible tales of what had happened. The monster was as big as a house! It had poisoned and mortally wounded the strongest and bravest man in the town!

"Just by snapping at him! Just by breathing on him!"

"Fancy that!"

"As tall as a church tower, they say the monster is!"

"With a loud and terrible voice! Like nothing you ever heard!"

"How shall we save the town?"

"Barn doors won't long keep in such a terrible creature!"

At last the mayor stood up on the steps of the fountain in the middle of the square.

"Listen, fellow citizens!" said he. "There's only one thing to do! We must pay the owner the price of this barn and of the hay and straw in it—we must pay for them out of the town funds. Then we must burn down the barn and the terrible beast in it."

And this is exactly what they did, except for one thing. Luckily for her, the noise and racket frightened Mrs. Owl so much that she bravely decided that she would face sparrows and daylight and all, rather than stay in such a noisy place where an honest bird couldn't get a wink of sleep. So, while they were busy fetching torches to burn the barn, and without anybody seeing her, Mrs. Owl flew softly out of a window high up in the barn roof. Then on her silent wings she soon reached her own hollow tree again, without being noticed by a single sparrow, and at last settled herself down comfortably to sleep for the rest of the day.

THE TWELVE DANCING PRINCESSES

LONG AGO, THERE LIVED A CERTAIN KING WHO had twelve daughters who were each more beautiful than the last. They slept in twelve beds all in one big room. Every night, as soon as the twelve princesses had gone to bed, the door of the room was shut and then it was locked by the King himself. And yet, every morning, when the King, their father, unlocked the door again, he could see that their slippers were all worn into holes, just as if they had all twelve been dancing instead of sleeping the whole night through. Not a word would any of the Princesses say about why this happened and nobody could find out where they had been.

At last the King, their father, sent heralds out to proclaim that, if any suitor, be he prince or peasant, could discover the secret, and could find out where it was that the Princesses danced, he should not only have the one he liked best for his wife, but should also, in due time, inherit the Kingdom. They could try three times, but, after three days and three nights, whoever had tried and failed would be put to death.

The first to try his luck was a King's son. He was well entertained, and on the evening when he said he was ready to begin the trial, he was taken to a room that led out of the one into which the Princesses were locked every evening. There he was to sit and watch, so that nothing might happen without his being able to see and hear it. But, oh dear, it wasn't long before the King's son fell fast asleep; and, when he woke in the morning, it seemed that the twelve princesses must all have been out dancing just as usual, for the soles of their slippers were just as full of holes as ever. The same thing happened on the second and third night; so there was nothing for it, and the King ordered his head to be cut off according to the bargain.

After this Princes, Dukes, Earls and many others came, but they fared no better—not one of them was able to find out the secret of the twelve dancing Princesses.

Now it chanced that one day a poor soldier, who had just left the army, came wandering through the country where this King reigned; and, as he was passing through a wood, he met an old woman who asked him who he was and where he was going.

"I'm only a poor soldier and I'm going to seek my fortune," said he civilly, and with that, the two of them sat down to rest. The soldier began to chat about the wounds he had got, and the hard times he had had in the wars and the poor pay. It was a sad tale, but he was a jolly fellow and he told it merrily.

"Is it true, Granny," the soldier asked presently, "that there's a kingdom and a wife to be won in this part of the country? They tell me that the one that is to win them must find out where twelve Princesses dance all night. Have you any idea how it could be managed?"

"Well," said the old woman, "it's really no very hard task."

"Others haven't found it too easy," answered the soldier, "but I must say I should like to try my luck."

27

"If you really mean to try," said the old woman, "the first thing is to take care not to drink any of the wine which the eldest Princess will bring you in the evening. But then, as soon as she leaves you, and when she thinks you have drunk it all, you must pretend to go fast asleep."

The soldier thanked her so nicely for her good advice that the old woman did something more for him. She gave him a little cloak.

"As soon as you put on this little cloak you will become invisible, and if you take great care and go very softly, you ought to be able to follow the Princesses wherever they go."

"Where do they go?" asked the soldier.

"See for yourself."

No sooner had the old woman said this than she vanished.

Well, as you can guess, after this good advice the soldier quite made up his mind that—though he knew what the bargain was—he was going to get himself a wife and a kingdom. So now he went straight off to the King, and told him that he had come to try to find out the secret.

Though he was only a poor soldier he was just as well received as all the Princes and Dukes had been, but as he was all tattered and torn, the King ordered a fine court suit to be given him. When evening came he was led, just as the others had been, to the room that led off the one in which the Princesses slept. Just as he was settling himself down to watch, who should come in but the eldest Princess: she spoke pleasantly to him and in her hand she carried a cup of wine. The soldier thanked her, but, instead of drinking the wine, he managed to pour it all away secretly, taking care not to touch so much as a drop.

Then he laid himself down on his bed, and in a little while he pretended to be snoring, and very loudly too,

The soldier pretends to be asleep

just as if he was in a deep sleep. The twelve Princesses had also been pretending to be asleep but really they were all listening and, when they heard how the soldier had begun to snore, they laughed merrily.

"This silly fellow will lose his life, just like the others!" said the eldest. "You see if he doesn't." Then they all got up and began to open their chests and boxes. Bustling about, chattering and laughing, they took out their fine clothes, and began to dress themselves at the looking-glass. Presently the youngest said:

"I don't know how it is, sisters, but while you all seem to feel as happy as usual I feel strange and uneasy tonight, just as if some bad luck were going to happen to us!"

"You goose! You silly young thing!" answered the eldest. "You're always frightened of something or other. Have you forgotten how many Princes and Dukes have tried to find out our secret and all in vain? And as for this foolish beggarly soldier, I do believe that, even if I hadn't given him the usual sleeping-draught, he would have slept like a pig!"

As soon as they were all dressed and ready, they tip-toed to the soldier's room to look. They could all see how he still seemed to sleep on, and didn't seem to stir hand or foot. Then the eldest Princess went softly back to her own bed and, standing by it, she clapped her hands, upon which the bed sank into the floor and a trap-door flew open. The soldier, who had got up quietly and was now watching through a chink in their door, could see how the twelve Princesses were going down through this trap-door, one after another, the eldest leading the way. As soon as the last was out of sight, he opened the door, threw his little cloak round his shoulders, and softly stepped up to the trap-door and found that it led down, as he had guessed it must, to a little winding stair.

As he followed them down, just in the middle of the stairs, the soldier accidentally trod on the long, beautiful train of the youngest Princess's dress. Instantly she cried out to her sisters:

"Someone took hold of my gown!"

"Silly young thing!" said the eldest. "I'm sure it just caught on a nail!" so they all went on down. At the bottom the soldier found that they were now outside the castle and in a delightful avenue of trees, whose leaves were all

30

made of silver, which glistened and sparkled. The soldier thought he had better take some token which would prove where he had been, so he broke off a small twig, but, to his horror, as he broke it the whole tree seemed to give a loud crack as if in warning. Once more the youngest Princess took fright.

"I am sure something's wrong," she cried. "Did you hear that strange noise? That never happened before!" But the eldest said:

"Pooh! It is only our Princes. I expect they are shouting for joy because they can hear us coming."

Then they came to another avenue of trees, whose leaves were made of gold; and afterwards to a third, where each leaf was made of glittering diamonds. As the soldier broke a twig from each kind of tree, the same loud warning crack sounded and each time the youngest sister trembled with fear. But the eldest still would have it that it was only their Princes, who were shouting for joy.

At last they all came to a great lake: and by its shore the soldier saw that twelve little boats lay rocking quietly with a handsome Prince at the oars of each. One of the Princesses at once stepped into each boat, the eldest Princess leading, and then, last of all, the soldier got carefully and soundlessly into the same boat as the youngest.

As they were crossing over the lake, the Prince who was rowing the boat with the youngest—the boat that had the soldier in it as well—said to her:

"The boat seems very heavy today! I don't know why it is, but though I am rowing with all my strength we don't get on as fast as usual."

"You feel tired with all this hot weather," answered the youngest Princess. "I feel it very warm too."

On the other side of the lake stood a fine castle whose

windows were all lighted up with lamps and torches, and the soldier could hear coming from it a cheerful sound of music. Horns, trumpets, and kettle-drums all seemed to be playing. As soon as they had landed they all went up into the castle, and here each Prince danced with the Princess that he loved best. But the soldier, who was of course invisible, had to dance by himself or not at all.

They danced till morning

However, each time one of the Princesses had a cup of wine set by her, the soldier drank it all up, so that when she put the cup to her mouth it was empty. The youngest sister was frightened at this also, but the eldest as usual told her not be so nervous.

Well, they danced on until three o'clock in the morning

and then, because their slippers were quite worn into holes, the Princesses were obliged to leave off, and the Princes rowed them back again over the lake. This time the invisible soldier went in the boat with the eldest Princess. On the opposite shore, each Princess took leave of her Prince, promising to come again the next night.

As soon as they had got back as far as the avenue of trees which bore the silver leaves, the soldier ran on quickly, got to the stairs before the Princesses, and laid himself down in his bed just as if he had never moved, and, as the twelve sisters, tired with so much dancing, came slowly up, they could plainly hear him snoring away in his bed, and so they naturally believed that their secret was quite safe.

Then, well pleased, they all undressed, put away their fine clothes, pulled off their worn-out dancing slippers and went to bed.

— 2 —

In the morning, the soldier said nothing about what had happened, because he thought he would like once more to enjoy watching such wonderful goings on and so, on the second night, everything happened just as before. The soldier once more poured away the wine and pretended to sleep, but once more he followed the Princesses.

On the third night, however, there was one difference. The soldier thought that he had better have yet one more token, so that the King would be sure to believe the strange story he had to tell, so, when the dancing was over, he carried away one of the golden cups under his cloak.

33

And now of course, on the fourth morning, the time had come when the soldier would have to declare the secret, and you can guess that he was careful to keep safely with him the tokens he had collected.

The King was ready on his throne, with all his court round him, and then the soldier was led in.

"Where do my twelve daughters dance at night?" asked the King.

"Your Majesty," answered the soldier, "I have discovered the secret." Then he told the King everything that had happened, first and last, about the Princes, the castle, the underground lake, and all, and then, to prove his story, he showed the King the tokens. He showed him the three twigs from the three avenues of trees, with silver, gold and diamond leaves on each, and last of all, he showed him the golden cup which he had brought from the castle itself.

Then the King called for the Princesses, and asked them whether what the soldier said was true. When the King had questioned them and when they had seen the tokens, they knew that, at last, their secret had been discovered. It was of no use to deny the soldier's tale and so they confessed it all.

Then the King, true to the bargain, asked the soldier:

"Which of them will you choose for a wife?" and he answered:

"I'm not very young myself, so I will choose the eldest." And they were married that very day, and the soldier was made heir to the Kingdom.

THE FOX AND THE CAT

ONE DAY MR. FOX MET MRS. CAT IN A GLADE of the forest. She was a small, pretty, black-and-white puss.

"Good day, Mr. Fox," said she, dropping him a curtsey, "how are you this fine morning? How expensive food is to be sure! I sometimes wonder how we are all going to manage! How do you get on these days?"

Mr. Fox was very proud, and without answering her polite greeting, he looked her up and down and then turned away his head as if he didn't care for the sight of her. At last he said:

"You poor, wretched bird-catcher! You hungry mouse-hunter! I'm never troubled about food being difficult to get! Fancy daring to ask me how I am getting on? How many arts and dodges do you know, you silly little piebald thing?"

"I only know one," said Mrs. Puss modestly.

"What art is that?" asked the Fox.

"Well, if the house dogs or the hounds chase me, I know how to jump up into a tree and save myself."

"Is that all?" said Mr. Fox. "I know a hundred arts and dodges! I've got a sackful of cunning! Really, little Mrs. Puss, I'm sorry for you."

Just then along came a hunter with a couple of hounds. Directly she heard them, the little Cat sprang nimbly up a tree and there she sat watching, gently twitching the tip of her tail. Right at the top she sat, among the thinnest twigs where no heavy creature could possibly catch her.

But poor cunning Mr. Fox! He was so long in choosing between the hundred ways he had of getting away from danger, that the hounds were on to him before he had done anything except think, so, as you can guess, that was the end of him.

"Poor Mr. Fox," thought Mrs. Cat, as she climbed quietly down from her tree when the danger was over, "he certainly had very bad manners! But I should have liked to have seen at least a few of his hundred tricks! But after all, perhaps it's really best only to know one."

THE SIX SWANS

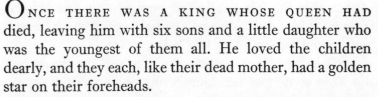

ONCE THERE WAS A KING WHOSE QUEEN HAD died, leaving him with six sons and a little daughter who was the youngest of them all. He loved the children dearly, and they each, like their dead mother, had a golden star on their foreheads.

Now one day this King was riding in the forest, hunting the wild deer. He chased a great stag so eagerly that it wasn't long before he had left his attendants far behind. On and on he galloped, quite alone, but when, at last, he lost all trace of the stag, he found that not only was he in a part of the forest that was strange to him, but that it was growing dark. What was he to do? He tried this way and he tried that, and the worst of it was that soon he found that he was always getting back to the same place. His horse was so tired that he could urge it on no more.

At last, as he sat bewildered, he saw, coming towards him, an old woman whose head nodded and shook as she walked.

"Good woman," said he, "can you tell me the way out of this forest?"

"Oh yes, Lord King, very easily! But it is a way that you will never find by yourself, and I will only show it to you on one condition."

"What kind of condition is that?" asked the King.

"I have a beautiful daughter," said the old witch. "She is as beautiful as any maiden in the land and well deserves to be your Queen. Agree to marry her and I will show you the way! If you refuse you will never get out."

"Lead on," answered the King, "and let me at least see this daughter of yours that you say is so beautiful."

So, with the old witch going before and the King leading his tired horse, they soon reached a little hut. There, by the fire, sat one of the most beautiful young women that the King had ever seen. She rose gracefully from her place, just as if she had been expecting him and she greeted him in a soft low voice.

And yet, beautiful as she was, and sweetly as she spoke, the King could not help shuddering as he stood there in the hut and indeed, for a moment or two, he could hardly bear to look at her. But he said to himself that there was really no reason why he should feel like this, and he thought his shuddering must be because of his weariness and the fear he had been in when he found that he was lost in the forest.

The end of it was that the King agreed to the bargain. He would make the beautiful young woman his Queen. He promised that if the old witch would show him the way now, he would come back to fetch his bride as soon as the wedding could be arranged. Then he said farewell and the old woman showed him a quick and easy way back to his own palace.

Now a promise is a promise. Yet still the King did not feel easy in his mind. How could he be sure that the beautiful Queen that he was going to bring home would be good to his children? So he resolved to put them somewhere where he could be sure that they would be out of harm's way. He remembered that he had a castle that lay in a lonely place and was indeed so hard to find that he would scarcely have been able to get to it himself if it had not been that a wise woman had given him a magic ball of yarn. When he threw this ball it would roll along the right path, so that, if he held the end in his hand, he could always find the place.

So, before the wedding, and before he brought home the bride, the children had all been hidden away.

Now the King loved his children very much, so that he often wanted to visit them, and so it was not long before the new Queen noticed that, on one excuse or another, her husband was always riding off alone, and she could not rest till she knew what his secret was.

The Queen offered great sums of money to this servant and that, and at last one of them took the bribe and not only told her about the six sons, but also that the castle where the King had hidden them could only be found by means of the magic ball of yarn.

The wicked Queen said nothing to her husband about what she had found out, but, in secret, she sewed six little shirts of white silk and, having learned many magic arts from her mother the witch, she sewed a charm into each.

Now it happened that the servant had said nothing about the little girl, so, when the six silk shirts were finished, the Queen imagined that, as soon as she could find the ball of yarn, everything would be ready.

At last she managed to discover where the King kept the magic ball, and, watching her opportunity, she took it from its hiding-place, put the little shirts over her arm and, throwing the ball before her, off she set, and it wasn't long before she saw a castle in the distance. The young Princes happened to be watching and when they saw that someone was moving, as usual, on the lonely path that led to their hiding-place, they supposed that it must be their father, so that all six ran joyfully out. But alas! As each came up, the wicked Queen threw one of the little shirts over him, and no sooner had she done this than each boy was turned into a swan which immediately spread its great wings and, first wheeling over

The shirts bewitch the Princes

the castle, flew far away—over trees, seas and mountains.

Now the little Princess had not run out with her brothers, but, from a window in the castle, she had seen that something was wrong, and then she had seen how six snow-white swans had flown over the castle. But the Queen, who knew nothing about a little sister, thought she had now got rid of all the children and went home delighted.

Next day, when the King went to visit his children as usual, he found no one there but the little girl.

"Alas, dear Father," she said, "they have all gone away and left me alone!" Then she told him as much as she had seen from her high window and she showed him six feathers that the swans had let fall as they flew wheeling over the castle tower.

The King could not believe that it could have been the Queen who had done this wicked thing, but what he did fear was that whoever it was who had done it might also steal the little Princess, so he wanted to take her back with him. But, though she had not been able to see everything clearly, the little girl felt very much afraid of the new Queen, so she begged her father to let her stay just one more night in the lonely castle. At last the King agreed and said he would come next day and then she must come with him.

— 2 —

But secretly the girl did not mean to go with her father. She meant to go and look for her dear brothers, and so, as soon as night came, she took a few provisions with her and went off alone into the forest. All that night she walked, and all the next day, and at last, when she was almost ready to drop because she was so tired, she

5

saw a little hut. There seemed to be no one about. The window was open and the door was not locked, so in she went, and, looking about her, she found that she was in a good-sized room with six beds in it. Not knowing to whom the hut might belong, she thought it best to hide, so she crept under one of the beds, and there she lay on the hard ground.

Just before sunset she heard a sound that she had heard once before. It was a strange sound, like a great wind, the sound that swans make with their beating wings, and, sure enough, in through the open window flew six great snow-white swans.

As she watched she saw that, as they alighted on the floor of the room, each swan began to blow at the other, so that, in a moment, all the swans' feathers had been blown off, and then she saw now each one stripped off his swan-skin as if it had been a shirt, and at last her six brothers stood before her. You can guess how delighted the girl was, for now she felt that her search had ended. She crept out from under the bed and her brothers received her with joy.

But soon the six Princes began to look sad.

"Alas, dear little sister, it's not safe for you to stay here much longer!" they said. "This hut belongs to a pack of robbers and if they come home and find you here, they will certainly kill you."

"But you would surely protect me?" said she.

"That we cannot do," they answered. "We can only lay off our swan-skins and have back our human shape for a quarter of an hour each day. You will see, in a very little time now we must be swans again."

At this their little sister wept and asked:

"Is it impossible to set you free?"

Then her brothers looked sadder than ever.

"Only you could set us free, little sister, but to do it would be too hard for you."

"Tell me at least how it could be done," said she.

At first they would not tell her, but at last she begged so much that they sorrowfully told her the hard conditions.

For six years she would have neither to speak nor to laugh, and during this time she would have to gather enough nettles to spin, weave, cut and sew six shirts, one for each brother, but if, during the whole long time, she spoke a single word, all her work would be lost.

All too soon the quarter of an hour was over and the brothers became swans once more, and flew out of the window.

Now the girl had at once de-termined in her own mind that, hard as the conditions were and even if it cost her her life, she would break the spell that bound her six dear brothers.

Only for a quarter of an hour

Stay in the hut she could not for fear of the robbers, so once more she went out into the forest, and there she found a hollow tree which would serve her as some sort of shelter. It was a tall tree and half way up it with a few branches she made a sort of platform. Here she slept, and, as soon as it was light, she went out and began to gather nettles. Then and there she began the long work, first spinning and then weaving. There was no one to speak to and, as you can guess, with the nettles stinging her hands she did not feel at all inclined to laugh, so it was easy to keep that part of the hard conditions.

There for a long time she lived, sometimes working outside the tree and sometimes on her platform, and all day she looked at nothing but her work.

— 3 —

Now one morning it happened that the King of that country was out hunting, and his huntsmen came to the very tree in which the Princess had hidden herself. She had heard them coming and she had climbed up to her platform where it was hard for them to reach her. They could indeed only just see her but they soon noticed that she was a lovely girl.

"Who are you?" they called.

But she made no answer.

"Come down to us!" they called again. "We won't harm you."

Still no answer, only a shake of the head, which made her golden hair ripple round her shoulders. When the men would not go away she threw down her golden necklace and then her golden girdle, then her dress, hoping that these things would content them.

At last she had nothing left but her white shift.

But they wanted none of these and, at last, one them climbed up to where she was, so that she had only just time to collect her yarn and her cloth before they carried her down and took her to the King their master. There she stood before the King as he sat on his horse, in her white shift and with her golden hair round her shoulders.

"Who are you?" asked the King, just as the huntsmen had done. "What were you so busy about in that tree?"

But she did not answer.

The King, amazed, repeated the same questions in every language that he knew, but still the girl was as silent as a fish. But the King's heart had been touched by her beauty, and it was not long before he felt that he couldn't be happy unless he took the lovely creature home with him. So he put his royal crimson mantle round her, set her before him on his horse, and rode off with her to his castle. There she was dressed in splendid robes, so that her beauty shone out like sunlight, but still not a word did she speak. She sat by the King's side as they feasted that night in the great hall of the castle and her gentleness and her modest ways pleased him so much that he said to himself that she was the only wife in the world for him. And so, after a few days, the wedding was celebrated and she became Queen.

Now till that day, the old Queen his mother had been chief lady in the castle. She knew well enough of course that one day a daughter-in-law would come and take her place, but she was not at all pleased that, instead of the daughter of some neighbouring King, her son should have chosen a girl that his huntsmen had found in a tree.

"Who knows," thought the old Queen, "where this dumb creature may come from? And what is this work that she is always so busy about? What is sure is that it is not fitting that she should be Queen."

But the King loved her, so for a long time there was nothing that the old Queen could do.

After a year had passed, the young Queen brought her first child into the world, and, as it happened, the little boy was born just when the King was away in another part of his Kingdom. This was just the opportunity for which the old Queen had been waiting. She took the baby away while the young Queen was sleeping, smeared her lips with blood, and when the King came back told him that his wife had made away with the baby. Fortunately the King would not believe such a tale. But the young Queen of course, could say nothing to tell him that she was innocent. Indeed it did seem strange to the King that she still seemed to care for nothing but the extraordinary work with which her hands were busy all day long and that when she went out, it was never flowers, but always nettles that she gathered.

After another year had passed the young Queen bore a little daughter and the very same thing happened. But when the third time came, and her baby again disappeared, all the wise men of the kingdom grew uneasy. The old Queen still told the same tale. She declared that it was the young Queen who made away with her own babies. So at last she made everyone believe that the young Queen was not only a witch, but a man-eater. As before, not a word could the poor young Queen say to protest her innocence. So at last the King, with a heavy heart, delivered her over to the judges. They tried her and condemned her to be burnt for a witch.

Now the day on which she was to be executed was the very day on which the six years were up, and the very day on which, if she had neither spoken nor laughed and if she had finished her task, her six brothers would be set free. She had not laughed nor spoken and she had almost finished. Only one sleeve of the sixth shirt was still wanting.

So, when the poor young Queen was led out to be burnt, she still had a little hope. She had laid the six shirts on her arm and, when she stood on the pyre and was just going to be tied to the stake, and when the torch was being brought to light the kindling-wood, she began to look around her. There was a great crowd, but because they were all sorry for such a beautiful young woman they were all silent. Then it seemed to her that, in this deep silence, she heard a sound that she had heard before, a strange sound, like a great wind, the sound that swans make as their strong wings beat the air. When she heard that, her joy was great, and it was greater still, when in a moment, six swans began circling in the air above her. As each one circled and swept towards her it sank low, so that she was able to throw one of the shirts over its head. Then feathers and swan-skins dropped off, and her six handsome brothers stood before her in their true shapes. Only the youngest brother, whose sleeve she had not had time to finish, had a swan's wing instead of a left arm.

Then the brothers all embraced and kissed their sister, so that the King her husband wept to see them, and for the first time, in all these years, the young Queen began to speak.

"Dear husband," said she, "you have seen what you have seen and you can guess my secret! I could not speak; if I had, my brothers could never have regained their human forms. Be sure that I am innocent of the

47

three dreadful crimes of which I have been accused."

Then she told him all the treachery of the old Queen, but as she told she wept for sorrow, because she did not know what had become of her three children. But the brothers in their swan shape had watched over them, and now three little children were brought to the King, and each one could be known to be the Queen's own child, for like her and her brothers, each child had a star on its forehead.

The wicked old Queen was punished, but the King, and Queen, their children, and her six brothers, lived for many years in happiness and peace.

RUMPLESTILTSKIN

ONCE UPON A TIME THERE WAS A MILLER WHO was not only very poor but also a great chatterbox. These were two misfortunes, as you'll agree. But to make up for them, he had a very pretty daughter, of whom he was very proud. He was so proud of her that he was always chattering away to everybody, telling them how clever she was. (They could see for themselves that she was pretty of course.)

One day he happened to have some business with the King, and when the business was finished, the miller's tongue ran away with him as usual, and he said to the King:

"That daughter of mine, your Majesty! She's so clever that, upon my word, she can spin straw into gold thread!"

Now this King was as fond of money as the miller was of talking, so, though at first he had scarcely been listening to the miller's chatter, he now began to prick up his ears.

"What's that you say?" said the King.

Whereupon the foolish miller repeated his silly boast and again told the King that his daughter could spin straw into gold.

"We'll soon see if that's really so!" said the King. "Bring her to me tomorrow morning."

Well, the miller wasn't sure whether to be glad or sorry when he heard the King say that. However, she really was such a very pretty girl that he thought that perhaps, if the King saw her, he might take a fancy to her, and even marry her.

So the miller went home and told the girl that next morning she was to comb her hair and put on her Sunday clothes and go to the palace, and, though he felt rather worried, he reminded himself that stranger things had happened than a King marrying a miller's daughter. Of course, as for spinning straw into gold. . . . But surely a clever fellow like the King would understand that this had been just the miller's fun?

Anyhow, next morning the miller took the girl, who was dressed all in her Sunday best, up to the palace, but he felt a bit frightened when he was told by the guards to leave her in the guardroom and to go about his business.

Well, the girl hadn't waited long before the King came in, and almost before he had greeted her, and quite without looking at her, he told her to follow him. He led her to a room that was half full of straw but had nothing else in it except a stool, a spinning-wheel and a lot of empty bobbins.

"Set to work now, my girl," says the King. "All this straw has to be spun into gold! Do it before tonight or it will be the worse for you!" and with that off he strode across the room. Still he didn't look at her, and what's more he wouldn't listen when the poor girl tried to tell him that she couldn't do any such thing, and that all this nonsense had just been her poor old father's usual boasting. No! The King didn't listen to a word of all that, but just went off, locking the door behind him.

Now what was she to do? She couldn't spin straw into

gold thread. She could only sit down on the stool and wish that her father hadn't talked such nonsense. The poor thing hadn't sat long before big tears began to well up into her eyes, and presently she began to cry in good earnest. Then it was that, between her sobs, she thought she heard a strange sound. She listened—the sound seemed to be a sort of scrabbling, low down on the door. Then she saw that the locked door seemed to be opening of itself. It opened just wide enough to let in a most extraordinary little black mannikin.

"What's the matter with you, my girl?" says the mannikin. "Why do you sit there crying?"

Well, she wouldn't tell him at first, for, after all, it had been too much talk that had brought her to this. But after a while, she thought that she couldn't be much worse off than she was however much she talked, and so, little by little, the black mannikin got the story out of her, first and last.

"What will you give me," says he, when she had done telling him, "if I do the work for you?"

"My necklace," says she.

Well, the little man seemed content with that so he collected some straw, motioned her to get off the stool, and at once sat down on it himself and pulled up the spinning-wheel. He span so fast and his fingers moved so quickly that the girl couldn't properly see what he was doing, and as for the wheel, it fairly whirred round! So fast did it turn that she couldn't so much as see the spokes. In a few minutes the first bobbin was full of something that shone and the girl could see that sure enough, the little black thing really had been able to spin a whole bobbin-full of gold thread.

As bobbin and bobbin was filled the wheel seemed to

51

go faster and faster. She couldn't even see his little feet now, as he worked the treadle, and it wasn't long before, to her amazement, all the work had been done.

That evening, when the King came back, he was very much pleased and rather surprised at what he saw, praised the girl and sent her off to be given some supper.

So far so good. But when she asked to be allowed to go home, she was told that the King had ordered a bed to be made ready for her at the palace and this, she thought, was not so good! She could guess only too well what might be coming next.

Sure enough, next morning, the greedy King came and took her to a much larger room furnished in the same way. There was just a spinning-wheel and a stool again, and this time a still larger heap of straw and a whole row of bobbins to be filled with gold thread.

Once more, when she was alone, the poor girl sat down and began to cry. Again she stopped sobbing when she heard the same scrabbling sound, low down on the door. Once more she saw how the locked door opened. And then the queer little man stood before her. This time she had to promise him the ring from her finger if he would do the work for her.

So that evening, when the King came in, and when he saw the gold, he was in high good humour. This time he even had a good look at the miller's daughter, as well as at the gold, and when he had looked at her he discovered something that everyone else knew already, and that was the fact that she was a very pretty girl indeed. However he said nothing about that.

She was given her supper as before, but, once more, she was forced to sleep at the palace.

Next morning back came the King and took her to a

yet bigger room, with still more straw and yet more bobbins in it, but this time as he left her, he said:

"All this must be spun by tonight! But if you can really do it, then you shall be my Queen!" The King had thought to himself, you see, that, even if this pretty girl was only a poor miller's daughter, he would never find a richer wife in the whole world than one who could spin gold thread out of common straw.

This time the girl had hardly sat down when in came the little black mannikin.

"What will you give me if I spin the straw this third time?" says he.

"I have got nothing left," says she sadly.

"No pay, no work!" says he, grinning, and when she heard him say that, the girl began to cry again.

Then the little black thing pretended to begin to think.

"If you become Queen," says he (after he'd let her cry for a bit), "will you promise to give me your first child?"

Well, as you can guess, the girl didn't like the idea at all —not of a bargain like that! But what was she to do? Besides, she thought, perhaps the King didn't really mean to keep his promise.

"Who knows if all that will ever happen!" thought she. So the end of it was that she promised the little man the reward that he wanted. Then down he sat, round went the wheel again, whirring faster and faster, till bobbin after bobbin was filled with beautiful gold thread and till, little by little, the great heap of straw had all disappeared.

Sure enough when the King came back that evening, he saw the bobbins and next day he really did marry the miller's pretty daughter, so that she became Queen.

And now she had a glorious time, for there was many a

feast and ball at the palace. A whole year passed, and the new young Queen had almost forgotten all about the funny little black mannikin. Indeed she never gave a thought to her promise, or him, until the day came when a baby was born to her.

Then, as she held her child in her arms, she began to remember, but still she hoped, as she played with her baby, that all might yet be well.

One morning however, very early, when she was quite alone with the child, the little man came to her room, reminded her of her promise, and then to her horror, he held out his skinny arms to take the baby. The poor young Queen clasped it to her breast and offered the little man all the riches of the kingdom if only she might keep her baby.

"No, you don't!" said he. "I don't want your gold! I would rather have something living than all the treasures in the world!"

But at last the poor young Queen held the baby so tight and she wept so pitifully that the mannikin said:

"I'll tell you what I'll do! I'll give you three days, and every evening I'll come back and question you. If, in that time, you can guess my name I'll let you off your promise!"

Now you must know that the little black thing belonged to the tribe of gnomes and that gnomes don't have at all the same sort of names as are given to humans. So, because of that, the little thing didn't believe for a moment that the Queen would have any chance of discovering his name.

Next evening when he came, he was grinning away to himself, quite sure that the Queen wouldn't have found out. She said every outlandish name she could think of. All through the alphabet she meant to go, beginning with such names as Aldebron, Balthazar, Caspar, and so on. But at every name she said, he only shook his head. At last she got to the middle of the alphabet and the little man said she had had her share of guessing for that evening.

Next morning the poor young Queen felt even more worried. She sent messengers far and wide, and by evening, they had collected all the names they could hear of. But it was still no use! Every time she said a name the gnome only shook his head and at each wrong guess his grin grew wider, till at last it stretched right across his face, from ear to ear.

Next day the messengers were all out again, but it seemed that all the names had already been collected!

But at last, late in the afternoon of the very last day, one of them—it was one who had been sent out on the first day and hadn't come back—came to the Queen in a great hurry, very muddy and breathless, and knelt at her feet.

"Your Majesty," said he, "as I came over the mountain, just at the place where the hare and the fox say good-night to each other, I spied a strange little house. It was a real house, but hardly big enough for a cat! In front of the house burned a fire and round the fire a little black gnome kept jumping and hopping about and singing. I have remembered the words of the song for you just in case they might be some use!"

"Quick, quick," said the Queen, "what were they?"

Then the messenger repeated the words of the song:

"Today I brew, tomorrow I bake,
    The next day I the Queen's child take,
  Little does she guess, poor dame,
    That Rumplestiltskin is my name!"

When she heard that you can guess the young Queen's

joy, and you can imagine how richly she rewarded the clever messenger!

All this was only a few minutes before it was time for the little gnome to appear again. There he stood grinning, but this time the Queen was ready for him. First she pretended to go on guessing at names, but then, at last, out she came with it:

"RUMPLESTILTSKIN!"

The little creature screamed out in a passion, and shook his little black fist at her:

"The Devil told you that! The Devil told you that!" And with that he stamped so hard that he disappeared through the floor, and the Queen never saw him again.

CLEVER GRETHEL

THERE WAS ONCE A COOK NAMED GRETHEL, who always dressed herself up very fine and who wore red rosettes on her shoes whenever she went out. When she walked down the road she always felt very much pleased with herself, and always thought what a pretty girl she looked. Then, when she got home again, she generally poured herself out a nice glass of wine, and drank it up, and after that she would sit down and eat a good plateful of whatever she fancied.

"After all," she always said, "the cook ought to know what the food tastes like!"

One day her master said to her:

"Grethel! I'm expecting a visitor this evening, so will you please roast us a nice pair of chickens for supper?"

"Certainly, Sir!" answered Grethel cheerfully.

So she plucked two nice fat birds, and got them all ready for roasting on a spit, and, towards supper time, she put them in front of a good hot fire to cook. She stood there, turning the spit to roast them evenly and, as they began to get brown, they smelt delicious. But the visitor was late, so Grethel called out to her master:

"Master! If the visitor doesn't come soon I shall have to take those birds away from the fire. But it will be a sin and a shame! They ought to be eaten now, while they are juiciest."

"Quite right, Grethel!" answered her master. "I'll go and see if I can hurry him up."

So off he went, and Grethel moved the chickens a little farther away from the hot fire.

"Standing by a fire turning a roast always makes one so hot and thirsty, and goodness knows how long they will be!" thought Grethel to herself. So she decided that she would have time to go down to the cellar and draw herself a glass of wine from one of the wine-barrels.

The cellar was cool after the hot kitchen and the wine tasted cold and delicious, so, while she was at it, she had another glass. Then she went up to see to the fowls again, for though she didn't want them to cook too much, she didn't want them to get cold either.

So now she put them closer to the fire again and, as she turned the spit merrily round, she basted them with butter so that they smelt nicer than ever.

"They certainly do smell good," thought Grethel. "I think I ought to make sure that they taste as good as they smell," and with that she began to lick one of her fingers. It seemed to her that the juice tasted even better than it smelt.

"Oh, how good a nice roast chicken does taste, to be sure! It's a sin and a shame to keep them waiting like this." And, shaking her head at the thought of spoiling good food, she went to the window to see if her master and his visitor were coming. But no, there wasn't a soul to be seen.

Now while she was at the window, and no longer turning the spit, one of the birds began to scorch and even to smoke a little.

"Dear, dear! I'd better get that scorched wing out of the way," said Grethel to herself.

No sooner said than done! She cut the wing off and ate it. Really, the scorched bit was almost the best! Looking at the chickens again, it seemed to her that a roast bird with only one wing looked rather lop-sided.

"I'd better take the other wing off to match," thought she, "or the master will think there's something missing."

So now Grethel had eaten two wings, and still the master and his visitor didn't come.

"Perhaps they aren't coming at all? Perhaps they've decided to have dinner at the inn? I'll just look out, and if they aren't coming, it really might be best if I were to have another glass of wine and then tidy that chicken up. After all, I can enjoy my supper just the same as anyone else! It's very wrong to waste good food, so I might just as well have a pleasant evening and make myself happy."

Well, after the whole of the first chicken was finished, Grethel, who was feeling more cheerful than ever, had another look out of the window. But still there was no sign either of the master or of his visitor.

Out of the corner of her eye, she looked at the other bird. It really seemed to her that this one was beginning to get over-cooked.

"Where one is," said Grethel to herself, "the other ought to follow."

She was just in the middle of the second fowl, when all of a sudden, back came her master!

"Dish up the chickens, Grethel!" he called out. "The visitor is just behind me! He'll be here in a moment."

Now what was she to do? What she did, was to answer him cheerfully:

"I'll dish up directly, master!"

59

The master, suspecting nothing, hurried through into the dining-room to make sure that the table was properly laid, and, thinking that the carving-knife seemed rather blunt, he went outside to sharpen it on the step that led up to the back door. No sooner had he shut the back door than the visitor knocked softly and politely on the front door. Grethel ran to open it.

"Hush," said she, putting her finger to her lips, "for Heaven's sake, Sir! Get away as quickly as you can! My master asked you to supper, but what he really means to do is to cut off both your ears! You can hear him sharpening the knife this minute!"

The visitor felt very much frightened at these words and, sure enough, when he listened, he really could hear somebody sharpening a knife. So only just thanking Grethel for her kind warning, he scampered off, back down the path, as fast as he could go.

Without even waiting to shut the door after him, Grethel rushed back into the kitchen, upsetting a hall chair and calling out as she ran.

"Master, Master!" she shrieked.

"What's the matter, Grethel?" said he, astonished, and then came in through the back door, still with the carving-knife in his hand.

"You invited a nice sort of visitor!" said Grethel, as if she was going to cry.

"What do you mean?" asked he.

"Why, he's made off with the pair of fowls that I'd only just dished up!" and with that she threw her apron over her head and began to sob.

"The brute! He might at least have left me one," exclaimed her master, as he rushed through the open front door. "Stop, stop," he shouted, running knife in hand after the vanishing visitor, "I only want one!" The visitor took one look. What he saw was the master

The master came running out

running after him with a great knife. Clapping his hands over his ears the terrified fellow ran as he had never run before. When he got home with both ears safe, he thanked his lucky stars and also kind, pretty, Clever Grethel, who had warned him just in time!

THE THREE GOLDEN HAIRS

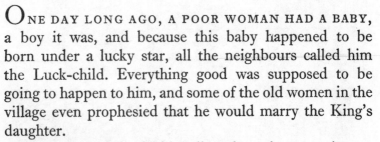

ONE DAY LONG AGO, A POOR WOMAN HAD A BABY, a boy it was, and because this baby happened to be born under a lucky star, all the neighbours called him the Luck-child. Everything good was supposed to be going to happen to him, and some of the old women in the village even prophesied that he would marry the King's daughter.

It was just while all this talk and gossip was going on about the birth of this lucky baby, that the King happened to ride through the village, and, because he came alone and disguised, no one knew who he was. He just seemed to be some rich man on a journey.

He asked the people he met what news there was in those parts.

"Oh," they said, "Mistress Brock, in the cottage down that lane there, has just had a baby that everyone calls the Luck-child. They say that everything will go right for that boy! They even say that, as soon as he is old enough, he is sure to marry the King's daughter."

Now this King was bad-hearted and proud, and he didn't at all like the idea that Mistress Brock's little boy from the cottage down the lane should marry anyone as grand as his daughter.

"I'll soon put a stop to that sort of thing!" thought he to himself, though he pretended to be very much pleased and interested. So, what did this King do, but go to the child's parents and, pretending to be quite friendly, he said:

"Why don't you let me bring up your child, you poor people? I haven't got a son of my own and the boy will have a better chance with me than he would with you."

Well, for a long time they wouldn't let the boy go, but they were very poor, while the stranger rode on a fine horse, was well dressed and seemed pleasant, so they thought that perhaps it was wrong to stand in the child's way. And besides he kept offering them a whole pocketful of gold pieces if they would let the child go with him.

"He's a Luck-child, everybody says so, so whatever happens things are bound to turn out well for him," they thought. So at last they agreed.

Now the King, as you know, was riding on horseback, and the best way to carry a baby on horseback is to get a nice little cradle for it, made rather like a box. The stranger managed to get one in the village and had a lid made for it as well, with holes pierced in it for air. The baby was wrapped up and put in, the lid was fitted on, the King strapped the box on to the back of his saddle, and away he rode, quite slowly, so as not to joggle the child. But no sooner was he well out of the village and had come to a place where the road came near the deep part of a big river, than he jumped off his horse, unstrapped the box, and pitched it, baby and all, into the water.

"Now," said he to himself, "I have freed my daughter! There's no danger that she will have to marry this beggar's brat."

But, as it happened, the box landed right way up in

the water. It was very well made and it didn't sink, but instead it floated like a boat. On it floated down the river towards the King's chief city till it was carried down a back-water to a place where there was a mill. On it went, right down into the quiet pool that always lies above a mill dam. By good luck the miller's boy happened to be standing on the bank.

He threw the baby into the river

"Ha! A treasure chest," thought he when he spied it. So he ran and fetched a hook and pulled it out, but when he had pulled off the lid, there, instead of treasure, lay a pretty little baby boy smiling and quite lively.

Well, of course, the miller's boy didn't really know what to do with a baby, so he took it to the miller and his wife, and, as they had no children of their own, they were very well pleased and took great care of the little foundling.

Years passed and the Luck-child grew tall and strong.

It happened one day, as the King was out riding, a storm came on and he went into the mill to shelter.

"Is that lad your son?" asked he of the miller and his wife.

"No, Your Majesty," the miller answered. "He's a foundling. It must be about sixteen years ago or more that he floated down to the mill-dam in a box, and the mill-boy that we had then, pulled him out of the water—box and all."

When the King heard that, he guessed what had happened and was very angry, but, once more, he pretended to be in high good humour and he praised the miller and his wife for their good deed in taking care of a little foundling.

"Could the lad take a letter to the Queen?" asked he. "If he will, he can have two gold pieces as a reward."

"He's at your orders, Your Majesty," answered they and told the boy to get ready. Whilst the Luck-child was getting his things on, the King wrote a letter to the Queen. In it he said:

"A lad will bring you this letter. As soon as he arrives have him killed and buried. It must all be over before I get home."

Then the King signed the letter, sealed it up, and gave it to the Luck-child with the two gold pieces.

The lad, of course, thought no harm, but was delighted with the money and set out as fast as he could, as proud as could be to be the King's messenger. But somehow he missed his way and, in the evening, there he was, lost in the middle of a great forest and he didn't know how to go on. For some time he wandered in the darkness and at last he saw a little light. He went towards it and saw that it shone from the window of a cottage. He knocked and when a voice had told him to come in he saw that an old woman was sitting by the fire, quite alone. She gave a start when she saw the lad and said in a frightened voice:

"Where do you come from? And where are you going?"

"I'm the miller's boy," he said, "and I am supposed to be taking a letter to the Queen from the King, but I missed the way and I've been wandering in this forest for a long while. Will you let me stay the night here? Then I can go as soon as it's light."

"You poor fellow!" said the old woman. "You've come to a bad place! This cottage belongs to a band of robbers and if they find you here when they come back, they'll half kill you as like as not."

"Oh, never mind!" said the Luck-child. "I'm not afraid, but I shall never find my way in the dark and I really am so tired I can't go another step." With that he stretched himself out on a broad bench that stood at the back of the room and was asleep in a moment.

It was not long before the robbers came back and they spied him at once.

"Who's that strange lad lying there?" the leader of them asked the old woman.

"Don't be angry," said she, "it's only an innocent lad who has lost himself in the forest. It seems he's on his way to take a letter to the Queen and, out of pity, I let him come in."

Then one of the robbers crept up and felt in the little pouch into which the Luck-child had put the letter for safety, and he passed it on to the robber leader. He opened it and read it and saw what was written in it. This, as you know, was that the boy was to be killed and buried as soon as he got to the King's palace. Then the robbers whispered together, and they agreed that it was a shame that a poor innocent lad should be treated like that. The end of it was that the robber leader tore up the letter and they all helped him to write another. Since they didn't like kings very much, they thought they would make the new letter as different as possible, so what they put in was that as soon as the lad got to the Palace he should be married to the King's daughter. Then they put the new letter back into the pouch, had their supper and lay down to sleep. Next morning, when he awoke, they gave the Luck-child some breakfast and showed him the right way to go on to the palace, so that he found it quite easily.

Well, the Queen was rather surprised when she had read the letter. However, there it was in black and white, and she did exactly as she thought her husband had told her to do. As the Luck-child was a handsome, well-mannered, nicely spoken fellow, her daughter, the Princess, was quite pleased with the match. It was a splendid wedding and the young couple started married life very contentedly.

You can imagine the rage of the ill-natured King when he got back to his palace and found that the prophecy had come true after all and that the hated Luck-child was married to his daughter.

"What have you been doing, wife?" he said to the Queen in a fury. "That was not the order I gave!"

Now luckily for her, the Queen had kept the letter,

67

and now she was able to show it to him, so that the King could see what was written in it. Then the King saw that he had been cheated out of his wicked plan and he called the Luck-child and asked what had happened and why he had brought quite a different letter.

"I know nothing about it," answered the lad, "unless it was changed in the night, when I got lost and slept in the forest."

The King flew into a rare passion.

"Luck-child though you are, don't think you are going to have everything all your own way! Whoever marries my daughter has to fetch three golden hairs from the beard of the Dark King who lives in the Black Mountain and who rules over the underworld. You won my daughter through a cheating trick, and only if you can bring me the three magic hairs shall you keep her."

Now the wicked King knew very well that this Dark King not only lived a long way off and in a terrible place but that he was a real man-eater. And he thought that even if the lad agreed to go, he would never see this detestable son-in-law again. But the Luck-child only answered:

"I'll fetch you the golden hairs! I'm not afraid!" He had always been a bold lad and now he had become very fond of his pretty new wife, and he did not mean to lose her. So, saying good-bye to her and telling her not to be afraid for him, he set out on his journey—and sure enough a long journey it was.

After a while his way led him to a large town which had walls round it and gates. When the watchman saw him he asked him what his trade was and what he knew. The Luck-child laughed.

"I know everything," he answered.

"Well, if you really know everything," said the watch-man, "you might do us a favour."

"What's that?" asked the Luck-child.

"Tell me why it is that the fountain in the middle of our market, which once flowed with wine, has now quite run dry, and doesn't even give us water?"

"All right, you shall know that!" answered the Luck-child. "Only wait till I come back."

After a while he came to another city and there once more, the gate-keeper asked him his trade and what he knew, and once more the Luck-child laughed and answered:

"I know everything!"

"Well, if that's so," answered the gate-keeper, "how is it that a tree in our town which once bore golden apples, now scarcely bears even a leaf?"

"Yes, you shall know that," answered the Luck-child. "You have only to wait till I come back!"

Well that was the last city he had to pass through, and next, he came to a wide river, and knew that he had to cross over it.

The ferryman was just as inquisitive as the watchman and the gate-keeper had been, and he too asked him what his trade was and what he knew.

"I know everything!" answered the Luck-child for the third time.

"Well then," said the ferryman, "be so good as to tell me why I have to be always rowing backwards and for-wards and am never set free?"

"You shall know that," answered the Luck-child. "Only wait till I come back."

Well, once he had crossed the water he hadn't far to go before he found himself quite near to the Black

Mountain and to the place where the Dark King lived.
It was a horrible sort of mountain and the Dark King's
dwelling was nothing but a great cave, which was black
and sooty inside.

The Dark King was not at home, but his old grandmother was there, sitting by the fireside in a big armchair.

"What do you want?" asked the old woman.

The Luck-child noticed that though she lived in such

a horrible place, she didn't look so very wicked, so it was
not long before he had told her his story and how, unless
he got the three golden hairs from the Dark King's beard,
he wouldn't be allowed to go back to his wife the Princess.

"Humf!" said the old woman. "You're asking for a
good deal, my lad! If my grandson the Dark King comes
home and finds you still here, I can tell you that it may
cost you your life. But really I'm sorry for you, separated

like that from your young wife! I've a good mind to see if I can't help you."

The end of it was that the old woman changed the Luck-child into an ant and there he sat on the palm of her hand, and he made signs to her that he wanted to ask something further.

"What is it now?" asked she.

"There are three things I want to know," answered he. "Why, in a certain town, does a fountain which once flowed with wine, now not even give water? Why, in another city, does a tree which once bore golden apples, now scarcely bear even a leaf? Also, why does the ferry-man on the broad river that I crossed on my way here always have to row backwards and forwards and is never set free?"

"Those are three very difficult questions," answered the Dark King's grandmother, "but if anyone can answer them, it would be my grandson. You keep quiet and just you listen carefully to what he says each time I pull out one of the three golden hairs. And now you must creep into the folds of my dress."

He hadn't been hidden long before the Dark King came home, and an ugly monster he was too. As soon as he got into the cave he began sniffing about.

"I smell man's flesh!" said he. "There's something wrong here!" and then he began prying into every corner and turning things over in his search.

His grandmother began to scold him. "What a nuisance you are," said she, "I have just swept everything clean and tidied everything up, and now you go upsetting it all again! You're always fussing about man's flesh! Sit down quietly and eat your supper!"

Well, after a while when he couldn't find anything, he

sat down and he ate a huge supper, and when he had finished he stretched himself out on a bench that was near the great armchair in which his grandmother sat. Soon he was fast asleep, snoring away with his head on his grandmother's lap. As soon as she was sure that he was sleeping soundly, the old woman took hold of one golden hair, gave it a sudden tweak and out it came. Then she laid it down for the ant which was hidden in the folds of her dress.

"Good Heavens!" cried the Dark King, waking up suddenly. "What are you playing at?"

"I've had such a dreadful dream," said his grandmother. "I must have seized hold of your beard in a fright."

"What was your dream?" asked he crossly.

"A very strange dream!" said the old woman. "I thought that a fountain in a market-place from which wine once flowed, had dried up and that now not even water would come out of it, and in my dream, I needed to know the reason."

"Why, that's easy enough," said the monster. "If the townspeople only knew what I know, they would soon cure that! There's a toad and it's sitting under a stone in the well that feeds the fountain. If they found that toad and killed it, the wine would soon flow again."

Well, it wasn't long before the horrid creature was asleep once more, and snored until the cave shook. Then the old grandmother pulled out the second hair and put it by the first, where the ant could get it.

"Am I never to have a moment's peace?" cried the Dark King, sitting up in a fury.

"Oh, don't be angry!" said his grandmother. "I must have done it in a dream."

7

She pulled out the last golden hair

"What have you dreamed this time?" he asked after grumbling a bit more and then lying down again and yawning.

"Well, it seemed to me," answered she, "that, in a certain kingdom, there stood an apple tree that used to bear golden apples and now there is not a thing on it, not even leaves, and in my dream I could not find out the reason for that."

"Oh, if they only knew," said the Dark King, "that tree has stopped bearing apples because there is a mouse lives at its root. The mouse keeps gnawing and gnawing. If they killed that mouse they would have golden apples again, but if they let it go on gnawing much longer, the tree will die! But I do wish you would stop dreaming! If you wake me up again I swear I'll give you such a box on the ear that you won't forget it!" This time he grunted and growled for a long time so that his grandmother had to sing to him and tell him stories for a long while.

Well, he did go off to sleep at last and once more he began snoring loudly. Then she took hold of the third golden hair and pulled it out, and put it with the others where the ant could get at it. This time the Dark King woke up in a rare passion! He jumped to his feet and started roaring and stamping about the place. But at last his grandmother managed to quiet him and then she said:

"Who can help bad dreams? This was such a strange dream too!" At last she talked in such a way that she got him quite curious as to what this third dream could have been.

"Well, you may as well tell me what it was," said he.

"I dreamed," said she, "of a ferryman who complained bitterly of his hard fate. He said that he always had to ferry passengers from one side of a wide river to the other, and that he was never set free. What do you think could be the cause of that?"

"Oh, that ferryman is just a fool!" said the monster. "He has only got to put the oar into the hand of the next person who wants to be rowed across the river, and when he has done that it will be the other man who will have to mind the ferry, and the old ferryman can jump ashore, as free as a bird!"

So now that the ant had at last got its three golden hairs and now that the three questions had been answered, the grandmother at last allowed the Dark King to sleep in peace. He slept till daybreak next morning and then he had his breakfast, and went off on his business. Then the old woman took the ant out of the folds of her dress and she gave it its human shape again.

"You have now got your three golden hairs, Luck-child," said she. "And I hope you heard what my grandson said in answer to your three questions?"

"Yes," said the Luck-child, "I heard and I remember!"

"Well, then you have got everything you wanted," said she, "and now go your way."

He thanked the old woman most heartily for the way in which she had helped him in his need, and after that, he set off on his journey back, and glad he was to leave the Black Mountain and the Dark King's horrible cave.

When he got to the river the ferryman wanted to know the answer to his question.

"Ferry me across first!" said the Luck-child, and when he was safely across the river and ashore he told the ferryman:

"Next time anyone comes and wants to be ferried over, you have only got to put the oar into his hand and to jump ashore yourself."

So the Luck-child went on till he came to the city where the apple tree stood, and of course the gate-keeper also wanted an answer, so the Luck-child told him:

"Kill the mouse that gnaws at the roots of your apple tree and you will get golden apples again."

The people of the town were so pleased now that they knew what to do, that they gave him, as a reward, two donkeys laden with gold.

Last of all he came to the town whose fountain had run dry. Here again he gave them the Dark King's answer:

"There is a toad hidden under a stone in the well that feeds the fountain. Kill the toad and your fountain will run with wine again."

Here too the townspeople were so grateful at having their question answered that they also gave the Luck-child two donkeys laden with gold.

So now he had four donkeys, each with a load of gold.

At last he got home to his young wife, the Princess, and she was just as glad to see him safe and sound as the King her father was sorry. The Luck-child told her the whole story, and to the King he took what he had been sent to fetch—the three golden hairs. He was careful not to tell the King the whole story, but what he did do was to show him the four donkeys each laden with gold.

"Tell me, my dear Son-in-law," said the greedy King, "where you got all that gold."

"Oh," said the Luck-child, who thought the King deserved some punishment for his greed and bad deeds, "that's soon told! I was rowed across a wide river and I found that, on the far side, gold lies on the shore instead of sand."

"Could I go and fetch some?" asked the King.

"As much as you like!" said the Luck-child, thinking that here was a good way of setting free a weary old man. "There's a ferryman on the river. Ask him to ferry you over and you can just fill a few sacks on the other side."

Now the bad-hearted King loved gold so much that he could hardly wait. He jumped on his horse at once and rode as fast as he could till he got to the river. Then he asked the ferryman to row him across. The ferryman told him to get in and, as soon as ever the King was in the boat, the ferryman put the oar into the King's hand, and jumped out on to the shore as free as a bird.

Ever since that time the King, as a punishment for his sins, has had to ferry people backwards and forwards across that wide river and some say that he is ferrying there to this day. So if ever you go that way, be sure that you don't take the oar out of his hand, however much he tries to give it to you.

SNOW - WHITE
AND THE DWARFS

ONCE UPON A TIME, IN THE MIDDLE OF WINTER,
when snowflakes fell like feathers, a certain Queen
sat at her window sewing. The frame of the window by
which she sat was made of fine black ebony-wood and,
as she sewed, and as she looked out at the fast-falling
snow, the Queen happened to prick her finger with her
needle. She said to herself:

"I wish I could have a little daughter with a skin as
white as snow, lips as red as blood, and hair as black as
ebony."

Well, it wasn't long before, sure enough, a little
daughter was born to her and, as the little thing began to
grow and toddle about, she was the prettiest little girl you
could wish to see, with a white skin, rosy cheeks, red lips,
merry dark eyes and shining silky black hair. What this
little Princess's real name was, I don't know, but what I
do know is that everyone called her "Snow-White."

Unfortunately, before her little daughter was grown
up the good Queen died and, after mourning her for a
year, the King married another wife. The new Queen
was tall and very beautiful, but she was proud and
haughty, and she had such a jealous nature that she could
not bear to have any woman or girl about the court who

might possibly be thought as beautiful as she was. This new Queen was an enchantress and she had a magic looking-glass, and she would often stand in front of it to admire herself. Then she would say to it:

"Mirror, mirror, on the wall!
Who is the fairest one of all?"

and the looking-glass would answer:

"Thou, O Queen, art fairest of all!"

Now the Queen knew very well that this mirror always told the truth, and as soon as it had said that, she felt quite satisfied.

But as time passed, and as Snow-White grew, she became more and more beautiful, so that soon she was as beautiful as the day.

When seven more years had gone by the Queen happened to look in her mirror as usual and she asked her usual question:

"Mirror, mirror, on the wall!
Who is the fairest one of all?"

This time the looking-glass answered:

"Thou art fair indeed, my Queen!
But fairer still is Snow-White, I ween!"

At this unexpected answer the Queen turned pale with anger, and almost fainted. Presently, in her rage, she called a huntsman before her and said to him:

"Take Snow-White away into the forest and kill her! I can no longer bear to have her in my sight!"

Well, the huntsman had to do as he was told, so he led Snow-White away, but when it came to killing her, he found he could not do it. So, instead, he left her by herself in the forest. Though he thought that most likely the wild beasts would get her, yet, all the same, the poor man felt as if a stone had rolled away from his heart because at least it was not he who had killed the pretty innocent girl.

Poor Snow-White felt very much frightened as she wandered all alone through the trees, but none of the wild creatures did her any harm. All day she wandered till she got to the very edge of the forest, and to where the mountains began. Evening had come, and she had begun to feel very tired and hungry. All of a sudden what should she see at the forest's edge but a tidy little cottage. She went up and knocked, and, at last, when no one answered, she opened the door and went in. Everything inside was shining and neat. There were seven small chairs, and on the table was spread a white cloth. The table was laid with seven little plates with seven little loaves on them, and the seven little glasses each had wine in it. Knives and forks to suit were all laid out in order, while, by the wall, stood seven tidy little beds.

Now Snow-White was very tired and hungry, so she picked a little piece of bread off each small loaf, and she drank a very little wine out of each glass, and, after that, what she longed for most was to lie down and rest. She tried all the beds, but she thought that one was too long, and another was too short, but at last, the seventh bed suited her exactly, and so she lay down on it and it wasn't long before she was sound asleep. Presently it grew dark, and then back came the owners of the cottage.

Now these were seven dwarfs, who worked all day among the mountains digging and mining for copper and gold. As soon as they had shut the door of the cottage, each dwarf lighted up his little lamp, and now, in the light, they soon saw that things didn't seem to be quite as usual. The first dwarf said:

"Who's been sitting on my chair?"

"Who's been eating off my plate?" said the second.

"Who's been eating my bread?" said the third.

"Who's been meddling with my spoon?" said the fourth.

"Who's been handling my fork?" said the fifth.

"Who's been cutting with my knife?" said the sixth. The seventh said:

"Who's been drinking my wine?"

Then the first dwarf looked round and said, "Who's been lying on my bed?" and each of the others had a look and soon saw that someone had been also lying on his bed. At last the seventh dwarf went to look and there, on his bed, with her black hair spread out on the white pillow lay Snow-White herself, fast asleep.

Then all the dwarfs brought their lamps to look at her, and when they had looked, they turned to each other with wonder and astonishment.

"What a lovely child!" said the eldest, and the others all agreed with him. They decided to take great care not to wake her, but of course the trouble was that now the seventh dwarf had nowhere to sleep. However, they soon thought of a plan. This was that he should sleep for an hour with each of the other dwarfs in turn, until the night was gone.

In the morning, Snow-White was rather frightened at her first sight of the seven little old men. But they asked her name and where she came from in such a friendly way that she soon told them her whole story. Then the dwarfs said:

"If you will take care of our house, cook for us, make the beds, wash, sew, and knit, and if you will keep everything neat and clean, you can live with us, and you shall want for nothing."

"With all my heart," answered Snow-White, and so she stayed with them.

— 2 —

Every morning the seven dwarfs all went to their work in the mountains and mined for copper and gold. Every evening they came back in time for supper. This meant of course that Snow-White was alone the whole day, and the good dwarfs, who knew her story, often warned her.

"Beware of your stepmother!" they would say. "She is certain, sooner or later, to find out that you are here; so be sure never to let anyone come in."

But the Queen of course thought that Snow-White was dead, and so, once more, she felt sure that she was once again the most beautiful lady in the land. But one day she went to the looking-glass and said:

> "Mirror, mirror, on the wall!
> Who is the fairest one of all?"

and the glass answered:

> "O Queen, thou art fairest of all I see,
> But over the hills, where the seven dwarfs dwell,
> Snow-White is still alive and well,
> And none is so fair as she."

At this the Queen was very much astonished and also very angry, but there could be no doubt about it, for she knew that the looking-glass always spoke the truth. She could not bear to know that anyone was more beautiful than she, and she resolved that, come what might, she would find out some way of killing Snow-White. She meant to make sure that there would be no mistake this time, and so she decided that she would do the deed herself. So one day she set out. She had painted her face brown and had dressed herself like an old pedlar-woman, and no one could have known her. In this disguise she went by a secret way and she had to cross seven mountains. But at last she came to the little house where the

The Queen and her looking-glass

dwarfs lived. Then she knocked at the door and called out in a disguised voice:

"Pretty things to sell! Come buy! Come buy! Very cheap! Very cheap!"

Snow-White, who was glad to have some one to talk to, looked out of the window and answered:

"Good-day, my good woman! What have you got in your pedlar's pack?"

"Good things, pretty things," the pretended pedlar answered. "Ribbons and laces to lace up your bodice, see how pretty!" and she pulled out a long lace—rather like a shoe-lace it was, but twice as long and plaited out of bright-coloured silk, with a pretty silver tag at each end.

"Surely I can let in the good harmless old pedlar-woman?" thought Snow-White to herself, and with that she unbolted the door, let the old woman come in and set down her basket, and, after a little chat, Snow-White bought the long pretty coloured lace.

"Child," said the pretended pedlar-woman, "what an untidy fright you look. Let me just lace your bodice up properly!"

Snow-White had no suspicion, but stood before her, and the old woman took out the old lace and laced her up with the pretty new one. But the wicked Queen laced so quickly, and she laced so tightly, that Snow-White couldn't breathe and fell down in a faint, as if she were dead.

"*Now* I'm the fairest of all!" said the Queen to herself, with an evil smile. Then leaving Snow-White where she lay, the pretended pedlar was off again in a hurry over the mountains, for she feared of course that the dwarfs might come back and catch her at her wicked work.

In the evening, the seven dwarfs came home as usual, and how shocked they were when they saw their dear Snow-White lying quiet and still on the ground, and when she seemed not even to be breathing. They lifted her up, and when they saw that her bodice was laced very tightly they cut the lace. Directly they had done this she began to breathe a little, and, after a while, she came to life again. When she felt better and had told the good dwarfs what had happened they shook their heads and said:

"That old pedlar-woman can have been none other than the wicked Queen! Take care, little Snow-White, and be sure to let no one come in when you are alone."

As soon as the Queen reached the palace again, she went straight to the looking glass and once more she asked,

"Mirror, mirror, on the wall!
Who is the fairest one of all?"

But the glass answered as it had the last time:

"O Queen, thou art fairest of all I see,
But over the hills, where the seven dwarfs dwell,
Snow-White is still alive and well,
And none is so fair as she!"

When she heard that, after all, Snow-White was still alive, the Queen's blood ran cold with spite and malice.

This time she worked for long at her spells and enchantments.

What she was making this time was a poisoned comb. It was a very pretty comb and any girl would have admired it and have wanted to wear it in her hair. But it was so deadly that only to touch it was almost enough to kill you. But the Queen, of course, could touch it freely for she was so wicked already that it could do her no harm. Then she dressed herself up again, in quite a different disguise this time.

Again she made her way to the dwarfs' cottage, knocked on the door and called out saying that she had pretty things to sell.

Snow-White looked out of the window, and this time she answered:

"Go away! I can't let anyone come in!"

"I suppose you can look?" said the disguised Queen and she picked the poisoned comb out of her basket and held it up.

Snow-White leaned out of the window, looked at it and thought how pretty it was. At last, when they had bargained for a while, Snow-White bought the comb and at once stuck it into her hair. Hardly had she done so, when she fell down unconscious.

"Lovely you may be," laughed the wicked Queen, "but you are done for now!" and once more she hurried away as fast as she could.

Luckily, the dwarfs came home early that evening, and when they found Snow-White senseless they at once suspected the wicked Queen, and it was not long before they found that Snow-White was wearing something new —the pretty comb—and they at once pulled it out of her hair. Hardly had they done so when Snow-White began to come round, and when she felt better she told them all that had happened. The dwarfs were very cross with her, though they were too frightened to scold her much. But they told her that she had been silly, and that she really must be more on her guard.

Meanwhile the Queen went quickly back to her palace and her looking-glass. How she trembled with rage when she got exactly the same answer as before, and learned that Snow-White was still alive. She vowed that Snow-White should die, even if it cost her her own life. That night she went up to her secret room in a distant part of the palace and with her she took an apple. It was a very pretty apple that was rosy on one side and almost white on the other. It was a very nice apple indeed, so pretty in fact that anyone who saw it was sure to long for it. She put poison in its rosy half, but the white half she left as it was. When this had been done, she dressed herself up again, this time as a jolly, fat countrywoman, and off she went once more with a whole basket of apples.

Once more she knocked at the door of the dwarfs' cottage, but Snow-White only opened a window and said:

"I can't let anyone in! The Seven Dwarfs have forbidden me!"

"That's all the same to me," said the woman, "I shall soon sell my lovely apples to someone else! Do the dwarfs really leave you here all alone all day? Poor child! I feel so sorry for you! I'll give you one of my apples!"

"No," said Snow-White, "I mustn't even take anything."

"Silly girl," said the woman, "what are you afraid of? Do you think that it's poisoned? Look! To prove that it isn't I'll share one with you."

With that, the pretended country-woman took a bite out of the white side of the apple.

"Take a bite, girl"

Snow-White longed to have a bite as well and when she saw that the woman had eaten part of the very same apple and had taken no harm, she stretched out her hand. Hardly had she taken a bite out of the rosy side when she fell down, as if dead.

Then the Queen looked in through the window at her and, with a dreadful laugh, she said:

"White as snow, red as blood, black as ebony-wood! This time even the dwarfs cannot wake you up again!"

Back she hurried to the palace and this time, when the Queen spoke to her looking-glass:

"Mirror, mirror, on the wall!
Who is the fairest one of all?"

the mirror answered, as it had, right at the beginning:

"Thou, O Queen, art fairest of all!"

Then the Queen's heart was at rest—as far as an envious and wicked heart can have rest.

— 3 —

That evening, when the dwarfs came home, they found once more that Snow-White was lying on the ground, quite still and not breathing. They lifted her up, and they looked and searched to see if they could find anything poisonous. They unlaced her bodice, they combed her hair, and they even washed her all over with wine and water. But alas! All in vain!

At last they laid Snow-White's body on a bench, and all seven dwarfs sat round it, and for three days and three nights the poor dwarfs watched and wept.

And now, they thought, the time had come when they would have to bury her. But, strange to say, she still looked as if she was living; and though she did not breathe, her cheeks were still rosy. The dwarfs hadn't the heart to bury the lovely girl in the dark ground, so they made a coffin of clear glass and they laid her in it so that she could be seen from all sides, and on the glass coffin they wrote in golden letters, "SNOW-WHITE", and that she was a King's daughter.

Then they put the coffin out on a rock on the mountain-side and took it in turns to stay by it and watch. The birds watched too, and they too wept for Snow-White, first the raven and then the dove.

And now Snow-White lay for a long time in the coffin, and she did not change, but only looked as if she were asleep, with her skin as white as snow, her cheeks as red as blood, and her hair as black as ebony.

At last one day a King's son came that way to hunt and when he spied the dwarfs' cottage he rode towards it, and, as he rode, he saw, on a rock on the mountain side guarded by a dwarf, a glass coffin with a beautiful girl in it. He stopped and read what was written on it in the gold letters. The Prince stayed that night in the cottage and all that night he dreamed of the beautiful girl. In the morning he said to the dwarfs:

"Let me have the coffin and what is in it! If you will do that I will give you all the treasure you ask."

"We would not sell it for all the world!" said the dwarfs, but the Prince would not take No for an answer. He said that he had dreamed all night about Snow-White and he could not live unless he could go on looking at this beautiful creature. He begged so hard that, at last, the dwarfs took pity on him and gave him the glass coffin and what was in it. So the King's son had the coffin carried down by his servants, meaning to take it home. Four of his huntsmen carried it on their shoulders, and as they went, it happened that one of them stumbled over a tree root. Then a strange thing happened. The shock jolted the coffin so that it almost fell on its side, and, as they righted it, the poisonous piece of apple came out of Snow-White's throat. Suddenly she stirred and opened her eyes, and then, when they had lifted up the lid of the coffin she grew warm again.

"Oh Heavens! Where am I?" she murmured, looking round with frightened eyes.

The King's son was full of joy and answered:

"You are with me!"

Well, it was not long before they had told each other all that had happened, and when the tale was ended the Prince said:

"I love you more than anything in the world! All night long I dreamed of you! Come with me to my father's palace, and be my wife!"

Snow-White agreed, said good-bye to the kind dwarfs, and away they went together to his father's kingdom.

The wedding was to be celebrated with great pomp and splendour and soon everything was ready. All the great people for miles around were invited, but no one was told who the bride was. One of the great people who was sent an invitation was the wicked Queen.

When she had dressed herself in her royal robes the tall and splendid Queen stood once more in front of her looking-glass.

"Mirror, mirror, on the wall!
Who is the fairest one of all?"

and this time the mirror answered in words that it had never spoken before:

"Thou, O Queen, art great in thy pride!
But fairer still is the new-made bride!"

90

You can guess how furious the Queen was at this. Who could the bride be? She hurried off in a towering passion of jealousy, and when at last she got to the neighbouring Palace, and saw that the bride was none other than Snow-White, the wicked Queen dropped down dead with rage.

But Snow-White and her Prince lived happily ever after.

THE MASTER-THIEF

LONG AGO, NOT IN YOUR DAY NOR IN MY DAY but in the very far off days, an old couple, who were very poor, lived in a little tumbledown cottage. One day a splendid carriage with four black horses drew up to their door. As soon as it stopped, a richly-dressed young gentleman, who was a stranger to them, got out of it. The gentleman greeted the old people politely, and asked them if they would be so kind as to let him stop to dinner with them. He added that, if they would agree, he would pay them well. The old people looked at each other, and then the old man answered that they were only poor folk and that, as usual, they had no food in the house that was fit to set before the gentry. But the stranger said that that was just what he had hoped, and that if they had some potatoes that would be enough dinner for him, for he had a special fancy for potato-balls, but that none of the grand cooks in any of the towns through which he had travelled knew how to make such things properly. So the end of it was that the old wife went into the kitchen, set on some water to heat, and began to peel and boil the potatoes, ready for making the potato-balls.

While she was busy over this, the old man and the strange gentleman strolled out into the orchard where the old man had already dug some holes ready to plant some new young apple trees; and, while the gentleman strolled about, the old man went on with his work. Soon the stranger began to watch him as, holding each young tree straight, he would fill in the hole and then tramp down the earth firmly round it. Then he would drive in a good stake beside each little tree and tie the young tree firmly to it with a straw rope.

"That's hard work for an old man like you," said the strange gentleman. "Haven't you got a son who could help you?"

"Well, Sir, I did have a son," answered the old man, leaning on his spade and sighing, "but he was a wild contrary lad and never much good to me! He was sharp enough, but he never cared for work and at last he ran away from home, and now his mother and I don't know what has become of him."

Presently the gentleman had another question.

"Why do you tramp down the earth round the roots of each of these young trees and then tie it to one of those upright stakes?"

The old man smiled, for he thought that great folk didn't know much about tree-planting.

"Why, sir," said he, "I do all that to make the roots firm and to make the trees grow straight! Trees must be trained while they're young."

"Perhaps your son would have grown straight too," answered the stranger, "if you'd taken as much trouble rearing him as you do with your young apple trees."

At that the old man only shook his head and sighed again. Neither of them spoke for a while.

"Would you know your son if he should ever come back?" asked the stranger after a time.

"Ah," said the old man, "it's true enough that he'll have changed a good bit! For of course for he was only a bit of a lad when he ran off, but even if he has changed, we should be bound to know him, for he has a little mark on his shoulder that looks just like a bean."

"Come into the kitchen a minute," said the stranger, and then, pulling off his coat and opening his shirt he asked:

"Was the mark something like this?"

You can guess how astonished and delighted the old couple were to find that they had got their lost son back again and to find that he had become a grand gentleman. But they were not quite so delighted when he told them how it was that he came to look like a lord and to be riding in a carriage drawn by four fine horses.

"When I left home," said he, "I fell in with a company of thieves and robbers, and soon I managed to do some work that surprised them."

"What was that?" asked his mother.

"I managed to steal an ox as it was being driven to market, and then the next day, and the next, to steal two more oxen from the very same man and then to let him have his beasts again, and all without his ever finding out who had tricked him! I ended up by stealing all the robbers' horses—stealing them clean away from the thieves who thought they were teaching me! So after that, I knew I had learned my trade and so I set up on my own as a Master-Thief. Those robbers never dared to do a thing to me, or to try to get their own back. They knew I could beat them at their own trade. So now I'm rich, and there are no locks or bolts that can keep me out. I just take anything I've a mind to. But don't be afraid! I never interfere with the likes of you! I only steal from rich people who have so much money they don't know what to do with it. Poor honest people haven't anything to fear!"

His father didn't like all this at all and he shook his head.

"No good ever came of such doings!" said the old man. But his wife said:

"Thief or no thief, he's still my son!" and when the Master-Thief had kissed his mother and given her a good hug, they all sat down to their dinner of potato-balls.

And now for a while they lived peaceably, with the Master-Thief sometimes lending a hand with the work and sometimes driving about in his fine carriage.

Now, not far from the cottage, in a very grand house, there lived a rich nobleman, a Count, who had so much money that he couldn't tell how much he had got. He had also got an only daughter and a smart and pretty girl she was. On one of the days when he happened to be dressed in his smart clothes and was out driving in his grand carriage with the four black horses, the Master-Thief caught sight of the girl. He got out of the carriage very politely and went over to speak to her and there he stood with his hat in his hand, while they had a few words together. The end of that was that they liked each other very well. He indeed liked the Count's daughter so well that he soon determined that, somehow or other, he would have her for his wife. So, the very next day, the Master-Thief said to his old father:

"I'd like you, if you please, Dad, to step up to the Great House this morning."

"What for?" asked his father.

"I just want you to ask the Count if I can marry his daughter," answered his son.

"You're out of your senses!" answered the old man.

"Nothing venture, nothing have!" said the Master-Thief.

"You can't be right in the head if you can talk such silly nonsense!" answered his father. "You just keep clear of the Count, or he's sure to find out all about the life you've led and then it would be his job to get you hung for a thief!"

"I don't mind what he knows! You can be quite honest about it, Dad!" answered his son, laughing. "Just tell the Count straight out what my trade is! But be sure to say that I'm not an ordinary thief, but a Master-Thief."

Well, you can guess that the poor old father didn't at all want to go up to the Great House on an errand like that! However, his son gave him no peace, so in the end, go he did. But when, at last, he actually stood before the Count, the poor old fellow was trembling and almost sobbing with fright.

"What's the matter with you, my man?" asked the Count.

At first the old man couldn't answer, but at last he told the Count the whole story—how his runaway son had come back looking like a grand gentleman; how he said he was a Master-Thief and how now he wanted to marry the Count's daughter.

But instead of being angry the Count only burst out laughing, and even patted the poor old fellow on the back.

"Don't worry!" said the Count. "We'll soon get the better of his impudence! Don't forget that if a man calls himself 'Master' of any trade, he has got to show a Master-Piece—a really good job—for all the world to see! We'll make your young rascal show us three Master-Pieces—just because of his impudence! Never fear! I'll make them so hard that he'll never dare call himself a Master-Thief again! Just you send him along to me."

Well, though he had heard the whole story, all the same the Count was rather surprised when a carriage with four black horses came up to the great house next day and when such a grand and well-spoken young gentleman got out of it.

"So I hear that you fairly frightened your poor old father and that you told him that you're a Master-Thief?" said the Count.

At that the young man bowed politely.

"And what's more, I hear that you want to marry my daughter?"

The young man bowed again.

"I suppose you're willing to show me what you can do?" asked the Count.

"It will be a pleasure!" answered the Master-Thief.

"Well," said the Count, looking very sly, "just because of your impudence we'll see if you can do three Master-Pieces."

"If it's thieving, Sir Count, I shall be delighted! Just say what they are!" answered the Master-Thief.

"First," said the Count, "you must try to steal my favourite mare from the stable."

"Certainly."

"But mind, I shall have a right to have her well guarded!"

"Oh, of course!" answered the young man. "Guard her as much as you like!"

"Then, on Sunday morning, you must steal the joint that will be roasting for our Sunday dinner out of the kitchen under my very nose, and just when the cooks are busy basting it."

"That won't be too hard," answered the Master-Thief.

"And last of all," went on the Count, looking slyer than ever, "on Monday night you must steal the sheet off my bed and the nightgown that my wife will be wearing."

"As you wish, Sir Count!"

The Master-Thief's grand carriage

"But don't forget," added the Count, "that if you can't do these three things, it's my business to catch thieves, and what's more to hang them!"

"Never mind about that," answered the Master-Thief pleasantly. "But will you, on your side, promise that if I really can do all that, you'll let me marry your daughter— and no more questions asked?"

"Yes! On the word of a Count!" and with that they both laughed. The Count laughed because he was quite sure that nobody in the world would be able to trick him three times over. The Master-Thief laughed because he enjoyed doing that sort of thing and because he felt sure that he would be able to do all that and because the prize was a pretty wife who fancied him already.

So now, when they had taken leave of each other, they each began to make their preparations for the first trial. The Count arranged that six of his grooms should watch the mare in turns day and night, three by three. The first groom was to hold the mare's bridle, the second was to hold her tail, and the third was to sit on her back.

After he had warned the grooms, and seen them all in their places, the Count went off well pleased, quite sure that, even this first time, he had set the Master-Thief an impossible task. Indeed he believed that the impudent young fellow wouldn't even try, but would drive away in his grand carriage, and take his boasting tongue far away and so, like that, he would trouble them no more.

Meanwhile the Master-Thief really did drive off in his grand carriage! But he only went to the nearest town and, when he got there, he just did a little shopping. First he bought some second-hand clothes from an old peasant woman, then he got some brown stain, then he bought a nice little barrel, then some wine to put in it, and last of all he went to an old man in a by-street who sold all kinds of drugs and medicines, and giving him a rather strange prescription, he asked him to make up half a pint of the mixture.

"Half a pint?" said the old man, when he had read the prescription. "It's powerful stuff, you know!"

"Yes, I know!" answered the Master-Thief.

Now, although it was coming on to Springtime, the nights were still cold, with a near frost, and when it got dark the three grooms (who had nothing to do except hold on to the Count's favourite mare in a draughty stable) soon began to feel shivery. It got colder and colder and quieter and quieter. Presently one of them heard someone coughing outside.

"Who's there?" called out one of them.

"Only a poor old pedlar-woman!" answered a shrill voice from the darkness.

The groom who was supposed to be holding the mare's tail took one of the lanterns and went out to have a look. Sure enough, there sat an old woman all crumpled up. She seemed to have been carrying a heavy load on her back for there it was beside her, and she was coughing and shivering pitifully in the darkness and cold.

"That's all it is," said the groom when he came back to the others. "Just an old pedlar-woman! She says she's got no bed for the night and asked me could she come in and lie down on the straw. It's just starting to sleet outside! It's no night for a Christian to be out!"

The end of it was that they let the old woman come in, and so in she hobbled, and she seemed so bad with her cough that one of the grooms had to help her with her burden. He noticed that the load seemed to be a small wine-cask.

"What have you got in your cask, old lady?" one of them asked when they'd had a good look at it in the light of the lanterns. But she seemed to be so deaf that they had to ask her again.

"A nice mouthful of wine," said the old woman at last

100

between coughs. "I get a living by peddling the stuff."

"A little of that would soon warm us up," said the groom who was sitting on the mare's back to the others. Then he said:

"What will you take in exchange for a glassful?"

"Money and good words," said the old woman.

So then he felt in his pocket and the other two grooms did the same, and, after a little bargaining, each of them bought a glassful. The wine was strong and soon began to warm them.

"When wine is good, I like a second glass!" said the groom who was holding on to the bridle.

"This wine really is old, I swear! It's as old as the old woman who sells it," agreed the one who was upon the mare, and he reached down his glass for another fill, while the one who held the mare's tail soon put out his glass too. So it went on, and it wasn't long before one groom decided that he could hold the mare's tail every bit as well if he was sitting down, or even lying down, while, as the bridle reins were long, the other groom soon had the same bright idea. So, as you can guess, these two were soon fast asleep and snoring. And now, somehow or other, the old woman seemed to have stopped coughing and to be much more active than before. Instead of hobbling she began to move about quickly and busily, but keeping in the shadows. Gently she loosed the hands that were still holding the mare's tail and gently she put into their grasp a wisp of straw instead, while the hands that had been holding the reins soon had a piece of loose rope in them.

But now, what about the groom who still sat on the mare's back? Peering up into his face the old woman could see that he had noticed nothing because he was sleeping as he sat. Nimbly the old dame unbuckled the saddle girths, threw a couple of ropes over a beam that was just above the mare's stall, tied the end of the ropes to the saddle and pulling hard on the free ends hoisted the groom up, saddle and all, and made the ropes fast to the posts of the stall. Who would have thought, half an hour earlier, that such a poor old woman with such a bad cough would have had the strength to do all that!

And now it was that the Master-Thief (for as you have already guessed, I'm sure, the old woman was none other) tucked up his petticoats, muffled the mare's feet by tying them up in old rags and, jumping nimbly on her back, rode her softly out of the stable. Out across the yard they went, and then, when they were well clear, he galloped her home to his father's stable.

It was when day was just breaking and when the Count was just getting up, and as he stood yawning and stretching as he looked out of his bedroom window, that the Master-Thief rode up on the stolen mare.

"Good morning, Sir Count!" called out the rider cheerfully. "Here's your mare! Do go and have a look in the stable and see how comfortable your grooms are!"

Well, it was a lovely morning, the mare seemed none the worse, and the Master-Thief looked so cheerful that, though at first he felt vexed, the Count couldn't help bursting out laughing. Presently, when he came down and took over his mare again, he even clapped the Master-Thief on the back. But all the same, as he did so, he said to him:

"Don't make too sure, you young rascal, that you can just go on playing me tricks! No! Not even once more, let alone twice! Remember, tomorrow is Sunday! The Sunday one is going to be harder! However, you needn't

102

try if you don't want to! You've still got time to use that fine carriage of yours."

"Thank you very much for the warning, Sir Count," said the Master-Thief and, this time, he pretended to look rather thoughtful, for, you see, he wanted the Count to think that perhaps he didn't mean to try the next thing, but would go off to where he came from.

— 3 —

As soon as he was out of sight and hearing, however, the Master-Thief began to whistle a cheerful tune. Off he walked to the village as fast as he could. There he managed to borrow a couple of hunting dogs, a net, and a sack, and then, with dogs, net, and sack he set off to the nearby mountain. By nightfall he had caught three hares, and had got them, all three safe and lively, in his sack. Then, once more whistling cheerfully, he returned the dogs and the net and went home with the three hares, very well pleased with himself, and had a good night's sleep.

Now, as the Count had reminded him, the next morning was Sunday. But though he meant to go to the Great House, the Master-Thief didn't put on his Sunday best. Not at all! He collected the oldest rags he could find, and where buttons were missing, he fastened these bits of clothes with odds and ends of string until he looked so poor and filthy that it made one's heart bleed to see him. Then, with his sack on his back, he stole into the passage at the back-door of the Count's house, just like any other beggar. The Count himself and all his household were in the kitchen watching the roast. Just as they were most busy, the Master-Thief let one of the hares out of the sack and it set off tearing round and round the yard in front of the kitchen windows.

"Oh, just look at that hare!" said the folk in the kitchen, and several of them were all for running out to catch it. Yes, the Count too saw it running.

"Oh, let it run," said he. "There's no use in thinking to catch a hare in the spring!"

It wasn't long before the hare found a way to get out and disappeared.

A while afterwards, the Master-Thief let the second hare go, and again they saw it from the kitchen. They all thought it must be the same hare that they had seen before, and now more of them wanted to run out and catch a March Hare, but at last this hare also managed to find the way out.

It was not long before the Master-Thief let the third hare go, and this one too set off and began to run round

and round the kitchen-yard, exactly as the others had done before it. And still they all thought it must be the same hare that kept on running about, and everyone of them was eager to be out after it.

"Well, it's certainly a fine hare!" agreed the Count at last. "And it doesn't seem to know how to get out either. All right, let's see if we can't get it!"

So out he ran, and the rest with him—away they all went, the hare before, and they after; so that it was rare fun to see. But the Master-Thief didn't waste time watching. Indeed he snatched up the roast and ran off with it; and where the Count got a roast for his dinner that day I don't know; but one thing I do know, and that is, that he didn't manage to get a hare to roast, though he ran after it till he was both warm and weary. That was twice he had been tricked!

So now, if the Count kept his word, there was only one more master-piece of thieving that had to be done before there could be a wedding. This was Monday's task, and what the Master-Thief had to do was to steal the sheet off the Count's own bed, and the nightgown that the Countess his wife would be wearing.

As they had done before, the Count and Master-Thief each began his preparations. The Master-Thief waited till it was dark; then he went to the gallows; there he found a poor dead prisoner hanging; he carried the body on his back to the Great House and hid it among the trees in the garden. After that he went and fetched a ladder which would be long enough to reach up to the Count's bedroom window. As for the Count, what he did was to get a musket, load it, lay it by his bedside and go to sleep.

Presently, when the moon was up, the Master-Thief got his ladder, set it up very quietly, and then with the dead man on his back, he climbed up it. He climbed just high enough for the head of the dead man to show at the window and then he made a bit of a noise, and he kept bobbing it up and down so that it looked for all the world like someone peeping in. The Count woke up.

"There's the Master-Thief," whispered he to his wife, giving her a nudge. "Now you watch me shoot him," and with that he took up the musket.

"Oh, don't shoot him after telling him he might come and try," whispered his wife.

"I'll shoot him all right!" replied the Count, and he took good aim. Next time the head popped up—*Bang!* The Count had shot the body of the dead hanged prisoner right through the head.

The Master-Thief, who of course had kept well out of musket-shot, immediately let the body go. Down it fell, down to the foot of the ladder, landing with a thump. As quietly and quickly as the wind, the Master-Thief ran down the ladder and hid among the bushes, while the Count, getting quickly out of bed, leaned out of the window. Sure enough there was a dead body lying on the ground.

Then the Count began to scratch his head.

"It is quite true," said he to his wife, "that I am the chief magistrate in these parts and that the Master-Thief had done plenty of crimes. But people are fond of talking and maybe they'll wonder why we didn't have a trial and all that. I believe the best thing will be for me just to go down and bury him quietly. So don't you say a word about it!"

"You must do as you think best, dear," answered his wife.

So now, down the ladder went the Count. He shouldered the body of the poor prisoner, and, taking a spade, he went off to a secret place in the garden.

No sooner had he gone and had begun to dig a grave, than the Master-Thief said to himself:

"Now's the time!" Up the ladder he climbed and in through the window and was soon in the bedroom. It was much darker in there than out in the moonlight.

"Why, dear, back already?" said the Countess, seeing a man standing there and thinking that it was her husband.

"Why, yes," said the Master-Thief, in a very good imitation of the Count's voice. "I just put him into a hole and threw a little earth over him. But just let me have the sheet to wipe myself with—he was all covered with blood and I have made myself in such a mess with him!"

So that is how the Master-Thief got the sheet!

Then he went to the darkest corner of the room, and pretended to be busy with it. After a while he said:

"Do you know I am afraid you will have to let me have your nightgown too. I'm in such a mess! The sheet won't get it all off!" So the Countess took off her nightgown and gave it to him. But now of course the Master-Thief had to think of an excuse to get away.

"Do you know, dear wife," said he, "I believe I must have left one of his feet sticking out! That will never do! To make my mind easy I'll just go down and make sure before I go back to bed again," and then off he went down the ladder and with him he took both the sheet and the nightgown.

He was only just in time, for now the real Count had finished burying the poor prisoner. Up the ladder he came and into the room.

"Had you really left one of his feet sticking out?" asked the Countess. "And what have you done with the sheet and with my nightgown?"

"What's that?" called out the Count.

"Why, dear! I'm only asking you what you've done with the sheet and with my nightgown! You used them to wipe off the blood," said she.

Well, though they talked till it was morning, neither of them could make out what it was that had happened.

However, once daylight came, they had not much longer to wait, for they were hardly up and dressed when there before them stood the Master-Thief, and what is more, there stood their pretty daughter with him.

Well, as you know, the Count and the Countess were the sort that can take a joke, and though the Countess felt a bit nervous as to what sort of husband her daughter was going to have, they had to agree to the marriage, for the Count had given his word. So now the two young people knelt before them and got their blessing. To tell the truth the Count wouldn't have dared refuse him now, for he was almost afraid that his new son-in-law would steal everything that he had, daughter included, if he did anything to vex him.

And that was how it was that the Master-Thief became son-in-law to a Count, and how he became a rich man, and how he got a pretty wife who loved him. I don't know whether he ever stole any more, but I am sure that, if he did, it was just for a bit of fun and that he gave back whatever he stole.

THE BEAR AND THE SKRATTEL

ONE EVENING, LONG AGO, THE KING OF NORWAY sat feasting in the great hall of his palace. They were drinking healths and the King drank:

"To our brother the King of Denmark!" and then he thought that he would like to send the other King a present. But what present?

Some said one thing, some said another.

At last Gunter, who was the King's chief huntsman, said:

"Send him, please your Majesty, one of our big white bears from the North, so that his subjects may know what sort of kittens we play with in Norway."

Now the King thought that this was a good idea because a white bear would be something new to the Danish king for they did not have any such beasts in Denmark.

"But," said the King, "how can we find a bear that will travel such a long journey willingly, and that will know how to behave himself when he gets there?"

"Your Majesty," said Gunter, "I have a glorious fellow! I got him when he was a cub. He is as white as snow, he plays with my children, and he will follow me wherever I go. He can stand on his hind legs, and he will behave himself just as a bear ought to do. I will willingly

110

take him to the King of Denmark whenever you choose."

The King of Norway was well pleased, and decided that his huntsman had better set off as soon as possible with the bear.

So Gunter went to his home in the forest, had a good night's sleep and, early the next morning, woke the bear, put the King's collar round his neck and away they went, on the nearest way to the Court of Denmark. Over lakes, valleys, rocks and seas they travelled, till they had not much more than a day's journey to go.

All this time the sun had shone and the birds had sung, and they had gone on merrily. But now the weather began to change and their way led them through a dark and gloomy forest. Whether it was that they lost their way, or how it was I can't tell; what is certain is that, towards evening, they hadn't managed to get out of the forest and that a cold wind had begun to whistle through the trees. There were big dark clouds that promised either rain or hail and it seemed that it was going to be a bad night.

Bear and master had begun to feel tired. What made things worse was that they had found no place that day at which to buy food, and so now they had nothing but half a loaf of bread between them.

"A pretty affair this!" muttered Gunter. "I'm likely to be charmingly off here in the woods, with an empty stomach, a damp bed, and a bear for a bedfellow!"

The clouds grew darker and darker; the bear shook his ears, and his master felt at his wits' end. At last, to his relief Gunter saw a woodman who came whistling along, walking by the side of his horse which was dragging a big load of faggots. As soon as the man was near enough, Gunter called out to him and was soon begging a night's lodging for himself and his furry "countryman".

111

Now the woodman was a good-natured fellow, but (as you know already) there are no white bears in Denmark, so he had never seen such a creature before, and neither had his horse which had begun plunging and snorting and rolling his eyes with fright as soon as ever he saw it. The woodman said he would gladly shelter Gunter in his hut, but as for the bear . . .!

"My wife wouldn't like a visitor like that," said the woodman, trying to quiet his horse and shaking his head as he looked sideways at the bear. "As like as not, he'd kill my dog and cat, not to speak of the ducks and geese, or else they'd all run away for fright!"

Well, Gunter begged hard, but it was all no good.

"If you and Shaggy-Back can't part, I'm afraid you must manage for yourselves, though you will have a sad night of it no doubt." And now the woodman couldn't hold his frightened horse quiet any longer so away he went through the forest, leaving Gunter and his bear to get on as best they might.

Gunter grumbled, and the bear grunted. The rain was falling fast by now and the two of them followed slowly along the track. Then, to their joy, they saw the woodman tie his horse to a stump and begin to walk back towards them carrying a faggot of wood.

"Oh-hoy!" cried the woodman. "I've had an idea! I can tell you where you can find shelter, but I warn you! It's a place where there has been a little trouble. It's my old house down the hillside yonder."

Then the woodman went on to tell Gunter how, quite near, there was a snug little house where he and his family had once lived well. But one unlucky night, a spiteful visitor had taken it into his head to pay them a visit.

"Ever since that night there have been such noises, such a clattering, and scampering up stairs and down, from midnight till the cock crows in the morning, that at last we were fairly driven out of the house. What the thing is like no one knows; for we never saw it, or anything belonging to it, except one little crooked high-heeled shoe that it left one night in the larder. We know it has got a hand (or is it a paw?) as heavy as lead. If it lays it on you it's as if the blacksmith's hammer had hit you. We call it 'the Skrattel' but what it looks like we don't know. If the linen is hung out to dry, it cuts the line. If it wants a mug of beer, it pulls the spigot out of the barrel. If the fowls are shut up, it lets them loose. It puts the pig into the garden, rides the cows, turns the horses into the hay-yard; and several times it nearly burnt the house down by leaving a candle alight among the dry faggots. Nothing stands still when that Skrattel's about. Dishes, plates, pots and pans, all dance about, clattering and breaking each other to pieces; and sometimes the chairs and tables seem as if they were alive, and dancing a horn-pipe. It's no use putting things tidy, for, in a few minutes, every-thing is sure to be upside down again. My wife and I put up with it as long as we could, but at last we couldn't bear it, so I built a sort of a hut for us—that's where I am going now. The day we moved, what did the little wretch do but help us off. On the morning we were to go we woke up to find all our goods put ready on the wagon and when we started we heard a laugh, then a sharp little voice cried out of the window:

" 'Good-bye, neighbours!'

"So now we live in the hut and that beast of a Skrattel lives in our snug cottage. If you and your friend like to sleep there, you're welcome. After all it may not be at home tonight," and with that the woodman gave Gunter the faggot of wood for his fire, went back to his horse, and was soon out of sight.

— 2 —

Well, anything seemed better than sleeping out of doors on such a night and, after all, if they did have to fight, the huntsman knew well that the bear, though he was so good-natured, could be an awkward one if anyone started a quarrel. This Skrattel (whatever a Skrattel might be) had very likely never seen a white bear before and, with any luck, might be as much frightened of him as the horse had been and might decide to leave them alone.

They soon found the house and a snug little place it was. The door was not locked, and there didn't seem to be anyone about. So bear and man walked into the kitchen and soon had a good fire going. But the worst of it was that they had nothing for supper except their own half loaf of bread. The wind blew and the rain was coming down harder than ever, so they sat by the fire and Gunter divided the dry bread fairly. After that he wrapped himself up in his cloak and lay down in the warmest corner he could find, while the bear rolled himself up beside the fireplace with his nose in his paws. Soon they were both asleep.

Now there was a clock in the house and someone must have wound it up for Gunter heard it strike twelve and, as the last stroke sounded, the door opened and in popped an ugly little Skrattel. It was smaller than a child of three, with a hump on its back, a face like a dried apple, a nose like a ripe mulberry, and nothing but a patch where one of its eyes should have been. It had on high-heeled shoes and a pointed red cap, and over its shoulder was a nice fat kid all ready for roasting.

The Skrattel brings his supper

Gunter lay as still as a hare and the bear never moved, but secretly Gunter watched. He saw how the Skrattel clattered about, here and there, blew up the fire, put the kid on to roast, rooted about in a cupboard that they hadn't noticed, pulled out of it a keg of beer, drew himself a mugful of it, laid the cloth and soon had the kid dished up and ready for eating. Then the little thing, in the joy of its heart, rubbed its hands, tossed up its red cap and danced about singing:

"Oh! 'tis weary enough abroad to bide
    In the shivery midnight blast;
And 'tis dreary enough alone to ride,
    Hungry and cold,
    On the wintry wold,
Where the drifting snow falls fast.

"But 'tis cheery enough to revel by night,
    In the crackling faggot's light;
'Tis merry enough to have and to hold
    The savoury roast,
    And the nut-brown toast,
With jolly good ale and old."

All this time the huntsman had lain quite still in his corner, rather frightened.

The little thing never spied him, but all of a sudden it saw something else; this was the bear's white back as it lay rolled up like a ball, asleep in the chimney-corner. The Skrattel crept softly nearer, not able to make out what in the world this could be.

"One of the family, I suppose," it muttered to itself.

Just then the bear gave his white ears a shake and showed the tip of his black nose.

"Ah-ha!" muttered the Skrattel to itself. "That's what she is! But what a very big cat! What shall I do? Shall I drive her out? I don't want a cat. I'm not afraid of mice or rats. I've thrown all the people and all the rest of the live-stock out of the house, so this one shall go as well."

116

With that it went to the corner of the room where there was an iron spit, just like the one on which the kid had been roasting. It stole back on tiptoe till it got quite close to the bear; then raising the spit as if it had been a club, the Skrattel brought it down *thump!* right on the top of the bear's snout!

The poor bear, who had been sound asleep, raised himself slowly up, opened his eyes, looked at the ugly Skrattel, shook his ears, and got up and padded across the room on his four paws. The Skrattel seemed a bit surprised, ran back a few paces and stood ready with the spit in his hand. Then the bear reared himself right up on his hind legs, came forward, and with one of his great paws, knocked the spit out of the little creature's hand, upon which the Skrattel gave a shrill scream of rage.

And now began a terrible battle; tables, chairs, pots and pans fell all about in the kitchen as they fought. One moment the Skrattel was on the bear's back pulling his ears and pummelling him with blows that might have felled an ox. Next moment the bear had managed to throw the Skrattel up in the air and then catch and hug it, so that the little imp squealed. Then it would be up again, jumping on to one of the beams out of the bear's reach and coming down, *thump!* astride on his back so as to hit him better.

Gunter was so frightened by all this that he crept into a cupboard, but still the fight went on, with biting, scratching, roaring, hugging, clawing and growling.

But at last it seemed that the Skrattel was getting weaker. The bear was just getting ready for another hug when, all in a moment, the little thing pulled off its red cap, dashed it right at the bear's eyes, darted to the door, and was out of the house in a moment.

117

Upon this Gunter scrambled quickly out of his cupboard, rushed to the door and bolted it.

"Well done, bear," cried Gunter.

So now, while the storm still raged outside, the two travellers sat down to the table, ate the Skrattel's supper and, afterwards, they both lay down and slept peacefully.

Next morning, as they started off on their way again, they met the woodman, who of course wanted to know what sort of night they had had. Gunter told him all that had happened and what sort of creature a Skrattel was.

"Let us hope," he said, throwing the woodman the red cap that the Skrattel had lost in the fight, "you're now rid of that gentleman! I suspect that he won't come back after the hugs he got, and if so, you're well paid for your hospitality which, truth to tell, was not of the best! If your ugly little friend hadn't brought his supper with him, we should have had nothing to eat!"

So with that Gunter said good-bye to the woodman and, if all tales are true, he and the bear reached the King of Denmark safe and sound.

— 3 —

As you can guess, the woodman and his wife kept a watch after that to see whether the Skrattel would come back to their old home or if it had been frightened away for good.

Three nights passed and nothing had been seen or heard of it, so they began to think that perhaps it might soon be safe to move back.

On the fourth day, however, while the woodman was out in the forest, he happened to shelter under a tree for

118

a while from a passing storm of sleet and rain. He stood very still and as he stood he fancied that he could hear a little cracked voice. It seemed to be singing, or rather croaking, a rather sad tune. Creeping along quietly and peeping over some bushes, he saw what seemed to be the very little creature that Gunter had described, none other than the Skrattel. It was sitting without any hat or cap on its head, with a mournful face, and with its jacket all torn and its legs scratched and smeared with blood. The woodman stood still once more and listened quietly to the words of the song.

> "Oh! 'tis weary enough abroad to bide
>   In the shivery midnight blast;
> And 'tis dreary enough alone to ride,
>   Hungry and cold
>   In the wintry wold,
> Where the drifting snow falls fast."

"Sing us the other verse, man!" cried the woodman, laughing.

The instant it heard his voice the little creature jumped up, stamped with rage, and was off out of sight in the twinkling of an eye.

That night, as he was going home, the woodman saw the little thing again. This time it was standing on a high bank by the wayside and it was looking as grim and sulky as could be.

"Is your great cat alive and at home still?" called out the Skrattel.

"My *cat*?" asked the woodman, puzzled.

"Yes! Your great white cat!" answered the Skrattel.

"Oh, my cat!" said the woodman, the idea suddenly dawning on him. "Oh yes, to be sure, she's alive and well and very pleased to see you at any time. And, as you seem to be so fond of her, you may like to know that she had five kittens last night."

"Five kittens!" screamed the Skrattel in disgust.

"Yes," said the woodman, "five! The most beautiful white kittens you ever saw. So like the old cat! Such soft, gentle paws! Such delicate whiskers! Come in tonight about twelve o'clock—the time when you always used to come and see us."

"I come? Not I indeed!" shrieked the Skrattel. "Keep your kittens to yourself—I'm off. You'll see me no more. Bad luck to you and your great ugly cat, to her five disgusting kittens, to your beggarly house, your silly wife, and to your horrible children!"

"And bad luck to you, Mr. Crookback," cried the woodman, and with that he threw over to it the red cap that the Skrattel had left behind in its battle with the bear.

So now the woodman and his family, with all their furniture, moved back to their snug little house and every evening the woodman, after supper, drinks a toast:

"Long Life to the King of Norway, to the King of Denmark, to Gunter the Huntsman, and most of all to the Wonderful White Cat."

THE SPIRIT IN THE BOTTLE

ONCE UPON A TIME THERE WAS A POOR WOODCUTTER who worked very hard from morning till night and managed to save some money. This he spent on sending his son away to a great school.

"Learn something useful, my son," said the woodcutter. "Then perhaps you'll be able to keep me when I'm too old and stiff to work in the woods any more."

So his son—whose name was Herman—went to the great school and a good student he was. He worked very hard, and stayed there a long time. But at last the money that his father had been able to save was all finished up, and even then Herman had not had time to learn all that there was to be learned, so he went to his father and told him how things were.

"Alas! I can give you no more," said his father, shaking his head sadly. "Times aren't so good now! Indeed I can scarcely earn enough to buy bread."

"Never mind then!" answered Herman cheerfully. "You've done quite enough for me, dear father. I'll stay here and work with you instead."

But his father only shook his head again, never thinking that Herman really meant it.

However, next day, when his father was getting ready

121

to go into the forest to chop and clear as usual, Herman said:

"I'll come too, and help you."

"Oh, dear son," said his father, "my sort of trade would be too hard for you. You are a student and have never been used to hard work. Besides, I've only got one axe and no money to buy another."

"Ask our neighbour to lend you one until I have earned enough to buy one for myself," said his son.

So this was done, and father and son went together into the forest. Though he had never done such work before, the student worked well, and was merry and lively into the bargain. About noon his father said they would rest now and eat their dinner, but Herman, taking his share of bread, said:

"You rest, Father, I'm not tired! I'll go a little way into the forest and look for birds' nests." But his father only said:

"Silly fellow! You shouldn't run about. You will make yourself so tired you won't be able to raise your arm. You sit down here with me."

But the young man was so pleased with the bright sunshine and being in the forest that, taking no notice of the old man's words, off he wandered among the trees, with his piece of bread in his hand, and, as he went, he peered about among the bushes looking for birds' nests. Presently he came to a huge oak tree—so big that five men, linking hands, couldn't have got their arms all round it.

"Many a bird must have built a nest in this tree," thought Herman and, as he stood still to look, he thought he heard a voice.

"Let me out! Let me out!" said the voice pitifully.

It seemed to the young man that the sound came from inside the tree. He listened again.

"Let me out! Let me out!" said the voice.

This time the sad little sound seemed to come, not from inside the tree, but from the ground, so the young man called:

"Where are you?"

The voice answered:

"Let me out! Let me out! Here I am, stuck among the roots of the oak tree."

So the young man began to search among the roots and, at last, half buried in a hollow, he found a glass bottle. He picked it up and held it to the light, and saw that there was something in the bottle that looked rather like a small frog and that jumped up and down.

The thing looked like a frog

"Let me out! Let me out!" cried the little thing again.

Then the young man, thinking no evil, pulled the stopper out of the bottle. Immediately the little thing sprang out and, as soon as it touched the ground, it began

123

to grow so fast that, in a moment, it stood before the young man like a frightful giant.

"Now I'm going to break your neck!" cried the horrible creature in a voice like thunder.

"Not so fast," answered the student. "My head will stay on my shoulders in spite of you!"

"Don't argue with me," answered the creature. "I'm the mighty Mercury, and whoever lets me out will certainly get his neck broken, for I was shut up in this bottle for a punishment."

"Gently, gently!" said Herman. "How do I know that you really were shut up in the bottle or that you really are the mighty Mercury? I shan't believe a word you say unless I see that you know how to get back into that bottle."

Full of pride, the horrible but foolish creature answered:

"Look then and believe!" With that, drawing itself together, it became as thin and small as it was at first and as soon as it was small enough, it hopped back into the bottle. In a moment Herman had clapped on the stopper again and then he put the bottle back among the oak-tree roots, laughing as he did it.

"Let me out! Let me out!" cried the creature in a small voice and even more pitifully than before.

"Not I!" said the young man cheerfully. "Not a second time! You said you were just going to break my neck!"

"If you let me free," cried the little thing, "I'll make you rich for life."

"No! No!" said Herman. "I tried to do you a good turn and if I did it again you'd be just as ungrateful as you were the first time."

"Indeed I won't be," came the voice from the bottle,

124

" It's really a very fine reward," it said

"I'll do you no harm, I promise you. I'll make you rich!"

Well, the end of it was that the thing in the bottle pleaded so hard and cried so pitifully that at last the student decided to risk it, so he picked up the bottle, and pulled out the stopper.

Instantly, the creature sprang out just as before, and in a moment was once more as big as a giant.

"Now you shall have your reward!" said the creature, and with that, what should it give the young man, but a piece of old rag.

"Is this the reward?" asked the student, not very well pleased.

"You'll find that it's a very fine reward!" said the creature. "Touch one end of it to a wound and it will heal it directly. Touch iron or steel with the other end, and it will change it to silver."

Herman decided that he had better try before the creature got away, so going to another tree, he sliced off a big piece of bark with his axe so that the sap began to run. Then he touched the place with one end of the rag, and immediately the wound in the tree closed up as if nothing had been done.

"That's all right!" said the student, nodding. "Now we can separate."

Then the Spirit thanked him for setting it free, and Herman thanked the Spirit for its present, the Spirit vanished and Herman went back to his father.

"Where have you been roaming to?" asked his father. "You seem to have quite forgotten your work! I told you you wouldn't do anything of this kind well."

"Never mind, Father, I'll make up the time," said Herman. "See, I'll cut down that tree at one blow!" and so saying, the young man took his rag, rubbed the borrowed axe with it, and gave the tree a powerful blow. But of course, because the head of the axe had now been turned into silver, it was quite blunt and soft, so all Herman's powerful blow did was to turn up the edge of the axe.

"Ah, Father, do you see what an axe you have given

me! It's got no proper edge at all!" said Herman, pretending to be surprised.

"What have you done!" said the father, who was frightened. "Now I must pay for the axe, and I don't know how; for it's the one which I borrowed for you."

"Don't worry, I'll soon pay for the axe," said Herman, but his father only answered:

"You simpleton! How will you do that? You've nothing but what I have! We've only got one axe between us now! This is some student's trick! It's clear that you know nothing at all about wood-cutting!"

"Anyhow, Father," said the young man, "I can work no more; let us make holiday now."

"Eh? What?" was the answer. "Do you think I can keep my hands in my pockets as you do? I must get on, but you may go home."

Well, his son pretended that he did not know the way because it was his first time in the forest, and at last he persuaded his father to go home with him, and even managed to talk him into a good temper again. When they got to their house, his father told Herman to go and see what he could get for the damaged axe. The rest of the money of course would have to be found somehow, so that they could pay their neighbour for it.

So the young man took the axe, and went off to the town. There he took the axe-head to a silversmith who, after testing it, laid it in his scales, and said:

"It's worth four hundred thalers, and so much I have not got in the house."

"Give me what you have," said the student. "I'll trust you for the rest."

So the silversmith gave him three hundred thalers and wrote down the other hundred as a debt.

The scholar went home and said to his father:

"Please ask the neighbour what he will take for the spoiled axe; I've got some money now."

"I know already what he's asking for it," answered his father; "one thaler and six groschen is the price."

"Better give him double! Two thalers and twelve groschen," answered Herman. "See here! I've got plenty of money," and with that he gave his father a hundred thalers, saying:

"You shall never want again! Live at your ease!"

"My goodness!" said his father. "Where did you get all this money?"

Then Herman told him all that had happened, and how he had made a capital bargain by trusting to luck.

And so the end of it was that the old father did live at his ease, but as for Herman he used some of the money to go back to the great school. Once more he studied hard, learned all that he could, and afterwards (because he could heal all wounds by touching them with his magic rag) he became the most celebrated doctor in the world.

THE GOLDEN GOOSE

———— ❦ ————

LONG AGO, IN GERMANY, THERE LIVED A COUPLE who had three sons. The youngest was nicknamed "Stupid" and was teased and laughed at by the whole family.

It happened one day that the eldest son took it into his head to go into the forest to cut firewood; and his mother gave him a delicious meat-pasty and a bottle of wine to take with him. At noon he sat down to have his dinner and had only just begun when a little old man came along and, after wishing him good-day, said:

"Give me a little piece of meat from your plate, and a little wine out of your bottle, for I am very hungry and thirsty!"

But this clever young man said:

"Give you my meat and wine? No thank you! If I did I shouldn't have enough for myself."

So away the little man went.

The young man soon began to cut down a tree; but he had not worked long before his axe slipped and he cut himself badly and had to go limping home. (Now it was really the little old man who had made his axe slip.)

The second son went out to work next; his mother gave him the same good dinner—a meat-pasty and bottle of wine. The very same little old man met him too, and asked him to give him something to eat and drink. But the second son too was far too clever to do anything of the sort.

"Whatever you get," said he, "I shall lose; so be off with you!"

The little man went off without a word, but he took care that the second son should have his reward as well, and at the second stroke the lad made with his axe he hit himself on the leg, so that he, too, went limping home.

Then Stupid said:

"Father, I should like to go and cut wood."

But his father answered:

"Your brothers have both lamed themselves; you had better stay at home, for you know nothing about tree-cutting."

But Stupid begged so hard that at last his father said carelessly:

"Have it your own way then! Perhaps you'll be wiser when you've suffered!"

As for his mother, who thought nothing of him, she only gave him some dry bread, and a bottle of sour beer.

Once in among the trees and before he had sat down to dinner, he too met the little old man, who said, as before:

"Give me some of your meat and some of your drink, for I am very hungry and thirsty!"

"I have only got dry bread and sour beer," Stupid said, "if that will suit you, you can have some and welcome. We'll sit down and share the dinner."

So they sat down. But when the lad pulled out his bread, it had turned into a beautiful large meat-pasty, and his bottle of sour beer had become delicious wine. So now the two of them ate and drank and enjoyed it all very much. When they had done, the little man said:

"Because you have got a kind heart, and have been willing to share what you had with me, I in my turn will give you something worth having. Do you see that old tree? Cut it down and you'll find the 'something' at the root."

So saying, the little old man took his leave, and went off among the trees.

Stupid set to work, and his axe never slipped in the least, so that it wasn't long before he had cut down the tree. When it fell what should he find, in a hollow under its roots, but a goose which had feathers of pure gold. He took the bird up, and put her under his arm.

Now as you know the people at home were never very kind to Stupid, so he thought that he wouldn't go back, but that it would be better to go out into the wide world to seek his fortune. So off he went. After a while, towards evening, he got to an inn, where he asked if he and his goose could sleep the night.

Now it happened that the landlord of this inn had three daughters; and directly they saw the golden goose, they were very curious to know what this wonderful bird could be. What they wanted most, of course, was to get one of the feathers out of her tail. They talked about this for a long time, and at last the eldest girl said:

"I must and will have a golden feather!" So she waited until Stupid had put the goose in a pen in the stable, then she quietly opened the stable door, crept up to the pen, and caught hold of the goose, meaning to pull out just one shining feather. But to her surprise when she had caught hold of it she couldn't pull her hand away, and there she stuck! As she was still pulling, along came the second sister.

"I can't get my hand away! Give me a pull!" whispered the eldest. But the moment the second sister touched her, she too found that she was stuck fast. At last the third came along, but this time the other two cried out:

"Keep away! For Heaven's sake, keep away!"

However, not being able to make out what in the world they meant, but seeing there was some sort of trouble, the third sister tried to help the others; but the moment she caught hold of her second sister, to give her a tug, she too stuck fast. And so they all three had to stay in the stable and keep company with the goose all night.

The next morning, Stupid came in, took not the least notice of the three girls but just picked up the goose and off he went. But the three girls had to come too for they were still stuck fast. Wherever he walked they had to follow, whether they liked it or not, and if Stupid hap-

pened to walk fast, they had to come along too, as fast as ever their legs could carry them.

Stupid led on across a field, and when they were in the middle of it, the parson met them; and when he saw the three girls, he shook his finger at them and said, frowning:

"Aren't you ashamed, you bold girls, to run after a young man in that way over the fields? Is that proper behaviour?"

When they didn't let go, the parson took the youngest sister by the hand to pull her away; but the moment he touched her hand, he too stuck fast, and was obliged to follow as well. Presently the churchwarden spied them, and, when he saw his parson running after the three girls, he too was very much shocked and wondered greatly, so he called out:

"Hollo! Hollo, your Reverence! You're wanted! Have

you forgotten that there's a christening today!" So now, up ran the churchwarden in his turn, and took the parson by the sleeve, and in a moment he was fast also.

So now there were five of them in a string, all forced to trudge along after Stupid, one behind another.

Presently, they saw two labourers with their mattocks, and the unfortunate parson called out to them:

"For pity's sake come and set us free!"

But of course this was no use. Scarcely had the two labourers begun to pull at the churchwarden's broad leather belt, when they too stuck fast. That made seven, all running and stumbling after Stupid and his golden goose.

At last they arrived at a city. Now it happened that this city belonged to a King who had an only daughter. The princess was so serious that no one had ever been able to make her smile, let alone laugh. Not long before, the King had proclaimed to all the world that whoever could make her laugh should have her for his wife.

As soon as Stupid heard this, he went straight to the palace and asked to be brought before her, still with the golden goose under his arm and followed by all these seven people. As soon as she saw the seven all having to follow, all hanging together, all running after Stupid and treading on each other's heels, she thought that they looked so ridiculous that she couldn't help laughing, and Stupid at once claimed her for his wife!

So they were married, and Stupid was made heir to the kingdom, and they both lived long and happily.

But nobody has ever told me what happened to the goose, the three girls, the parson, the churchwarden, or the two labourers. I only hope they all got home safe.

RAPUNZEL

Once upon a time a man and his wife lived in a cottage on the edge of a town. There was a little window at the back of their house from which a splendid garden could be seen, and this garden was full of beautiful flowers and herbs.

Now this couple had been married for a long while, and they had never had a child, though they greatly wanted one, but, at last, it seemed to the woman that their wish was going to be granted.

Sometimes she would stand at the window looking out into the beautiful garden and one day, as she stood, she noticed that there was a bed of very special herbs of a kind which we call rampion, and which in Germany was called rapunzel. The woman thought to herself that if only she could have some of the roots of this rapunzel to eat, it would be far better than radish, and if only she could have some of the leaves, she would like it better than the nicest lettuce.

That evening, when he came back from work, her husband could see that there was something wrong and he asked her:

"What's the matter, dear wife?"

"Oh," said she, "how I long for some of that rapunzel

135

to eat! There is a lovely bed of it in that garden at the back of our house. I feel as if I shall die if I don't get some."

Now the man knew very well that this garden not only had a high wall round it, but also that it belonged to a powerful enchantress of whom everyone was afraid, so he said nothing; but next day, seeing that his wife seemed to be quite ill, and was growing more and more pale and miserable, he decided that, dangerous though it might be, he would get her some of the beautiful green leaves and some of the fine white roots. So, in the evening, when twilight came, he climbed up over the high wall and down into the garden; then he hastily clutched up a handful of the herbs and took it to his wife. Quickly she cut up the leaves, and she sliced up the roots, and she made a salad of it. It was delicious!

But she liked it so much and it tasted so good, that soon she longed for it three times as much as she had done before, and so her husband, who loved her very much, once more managed to clamber over the high wall. But this time, just as he stooped to gather the salad he saw something that made his heart almost stop beating, for there was the old enchantress, standing right in front of him.

"How dare you climb over into my garden like a robber and steal my herbs," said she, in a terrible voice. "You are nothing but a thief and it will be the worse for you!"

"Be merciful!" answered the man. "My wife saw your beautiful bed of herbs from our little window and she felt such a longing for it that I really thought she would fall ill and die if I didn't get her some."

"Well," said the old enchantress, who was called Gothel, "if that is so, your wife can have as much of the salad as she likes, but only on one condition. She will soon bring a child into the world, and when that child is a month old it must be given to me. She need not be afraid for it! I will treat it well and will care for it like a mother."

Well, as you can guess, the man did not like such a bargain at all, but at last, in his terror, he agreed, and now every day his wife got the salad that she longed for.

After a while, a pretty little daughter was born to them, a beautiful baby. But on the very day when this baby was a month old, the enchantress appeared and, giving the little thing the name of Rapunzel, after the beautiful herb, she took it away with her.

Every year, till she was twelve years old, little Rapunzel grew more and more beautiful. Where she and old Gothel the enchantress lived, I do not know, but what I do know is that Rapunzel's sorrowful parents never saw her walking in the garden, though for years they kept looking longingly through the little window, hoping to catch a glimpse of her.

When she was almost grown-up, the enchantress took her away to a forest and there she shut the lovely maiden into a tower. A very strange tower it was too, for it had neither steps nor door, but only, almost at the top, a window.

When the enchantress wanted to come in she used to stand under the little window and then she would call out:

> "Rapunzel, Rapunzel,
> Let down thy hair,
> That I may climb
> Without a stair."

Now Rapunzel had wonderful long heavy hair that

shone like gold and, when she heard the words of the enchantress, she would open the window, unfasten her plaits, wind the top of them round one of the hooks of the window and then let the long shining hair fall down so that the enchantress might climb up by it.

For a long time the two of them lived like this, Rapunzel always shut away in the tower, and old Gothel the enchantress coming and going.

One day it happened that, as the King's son was riding through the forest, he passed near the tower and heard a voice singing. It seemed to come from the tower and was so sweet that he stopped his horse and listened. It was —as you can guess—poor lonely Rapunzel passing away the time by singing to herself.

Of course the King's son wanted to see the girl who sang so sweetly and so he rode round the tower looking for the door, but he could find none. Then he rode home, but somehow he could not forget the sweet voice or the thought that some girl lived there in loneliness in the strange tower in the middle of the forest. Soon it became his custom to ride into the forest every day to listen to the singing.

One day when he was standing listening (and well hidden behind a tree) he saw the old enchantress who was making her way through the forest, and when she got to the tower, he heard her call out:

"Rapunzel, Rapunzel,
Let down thy hair,
That I may climb
Without a stair."

Then for the first time, the Prince saw Rapunzel's long shining hair being let down from the little window, and at last he caught a glimpse of her lovely face.

"If that is the ladder," said he to himself, "I will climb it too and try my fortune."

The next day he came at dusk instead of in the morning and, standing below the window, out of sight, called out:

"Rapunzel, Rapunzel,
Let down thy hair,
That I may climb
Without a stair."

Down came the golden hair and the King's son climbed up. Now Rapunzel had had no idea that it was not old Gothel who had called her, and when a young man climbed in over the window-sill she was terrified.

Rapunzel was afraid when she saw the Prince

But the King's son was handsome and he talked gently to her and told her how he had come every day to listen to her singing and how he felt such love for her that he had been forced to take this way of seeing her.

At last Rapunzel lost her fear and when he asked her if she would marry him, she thought to herself:

"He will love me more than old Dame Gothel does," so she said "Yes," and laid her hand on his.

"I would willingly go away with you," said she, "but I don't know how to get down! Bring a skein of silk every time you come and I will make a ladder out of it and, when it is ready, I will get down by it out of the tower and you shall take me away on your horse."

So it was agreed that they should be man and wife and that he was to come to her every evening, because the old woman always came in the daytime.

And then at last, one day when she was with old Gothel Rapunzel said, without thinking:

"You climb up much more slowly than the King's son! He's with me in a moment."

"Wicked girl," cried old Gothel, "what is this I hear? I thought I had hidden you from all the world, and yet you have deceived me." She soon had got the whole story out of the terrified Rapunzel and then, in her anger, the old enchantress caught hold of the beautiful shining hair, wrapped it twice round her left hand, seized a pair of scissors with her right hand, and *Snip! Snap!* the long golden hair was cut off and lay on the ground. Then Gothel banished Rapunzel and took her away to a waste and desert place where she told her she would have to live from now on, in sorrow and misery.

Then old Gothel went back to the tower, climbed up by the golden hair that she had fastened to the window, and drawing it all up carefully after her, she waited for the evening. The King's son came as usual, suspecting nothing, and, standing below the window, he called out:

"Rapunzel, Rapunzel,
Let down thy hair,
That I may climb
Without a stair."

As soon as she heard him, the enchantress let the golden hair fall down.

What was the Prince's horror when, as he climbed in over the window ledge, he saw standing before him old Gothel, the enchantress, instead of his dearest Rapunzel. The old creature stood looking at him with her wicked, glittering eyes.

"Ah," she cried, "you came for your darling! But the pretty song-bird is not in its nest any longer. The cat has caught her and will scratch out your eyes as well. Your little wife is lost to you! You will never see her again!"

When he heard these dreadful words, the King's son was almost beside himself, and without thinking of the danger, he jumped straight out of the window, and fell right down the whole height of the tower, and the thorns into which he fell scratched his eyes so terribly that he could see nothing and had to feel his way. How could he possibly find his dear Rapunzel now? It really seemed that, as the wicked old Gothel had threatened, he would never see her again.

Thus, for a long time, the poor young Prince wandered blind through the wood, eating nothing, but weeping and lamenting the loss of Rapunzel.

Now Rapunzel, the Prince's lost wife, had found a little hut, and there had been born to her their twin children, a boy and a girl. At last, in his wandering, it

141

happened that the Prince came near to that very place just when Rapunzel was singing to their children. The Prince listened and, though he could see nothing, he recognized her voice and called to her, "Rapunzel! Rapunzel!"

Rapunzel looked up, and there stood a blind wanderer, all in rags. But Rapunzel knew him directly and fell on his neck weeping to see him so changed. But when her tears touched his eyes they became clear again, and it wasn't long before he could see his dear Rapunzel and his children, safe and sound.

So now, at last, the four of them went back to his father's kingdom, where he was received with great joy and there they all lived for many years, happy and contented.

HANS IN LUCK

Hans was an apprentice-boy, and when he had served his master for seven years, so that his time was up, Hans said:

"Master, now that I've learned my trade, I should like to go home to my mother. Please give me my wages."

His master said:

"You have been a good servant, so your pay shall be good too!" Then, what should he give Hans but a lump of gold that was almost as big as his head!

Hans pulled out his big handkerchief, put the lump of gold into it, hoisted it on to his shoulder, and with a bit of bread in his pocket, he trudged off homewards.

After he had walked a mile or two, he began to feel tired and was soon dragging one foot after the other. Presently a man came in sight, trotting along merrily on a good horse.

"Ah!" said Hans quite loud. "What a fine thing it is to ride on horseback! There that fellow sits as if he were on a comfortable chair. He doesn't trip over stones, his shoes don't wear out, and he gets on he hardly knows how."

The horseman heard this, and said:

"Well, Hans, why do you go on foot then?"

"Ah!" said Hans. "I've got this great lump to carry;

to be sure it's gold, but it's so heavy that I can't hold up my head, and besides the weight of it hurts my shoulder."

"I'll tell you what!" said the horseman. "I'll give you my horse, and you shall give me the gold."

"With all my heart," said Hans, "but I warn you! You'll only be able to crawl along with such a heavy lump."

The horseman said he would take his chance of that, jumped down from the saddle, took the gold, helped Hans up, put the reins into his hand, and said:

"When you want to go faster, you must click with your tongue and call out, '*Gee up!*' "

Hans was delighted to be sitting up there on the horse, and to be riding away so bold and free. After a time he thought the horse ought to go faster, so he clicked with his tongue and called out:

"*Gee up!*"

Away went the willing horse at a fast trot. But Hans fell off at once and what's more he landed in a ditch, and the horse would have trotted on on its own, if a young fellow who was coming along, driving a cow, hadn't stopped it. Hans soon picked himself up, and got on his legs again. He felt very much vexed, and said to the young fellow:

"This riding is no joke when a man gets on a beast like this, that stumbles and flings him off as if it was trying to break his neck! However, I'm off its back now, once for all. I like your cow a great deal better; anyone can walk along quietly behind her, and have milk, butter, and cheese every day into the bargain. I wish I had a cow like that!"

"Well," said the young fellow, "if you're so fond of her, I'll change my cow for your horse."

"Done!" said Hans, delighted.

The young fellow didn't waste a moment, but jumped on the horse and away he rode.

Hans quietly drove off his cow, thinking what a lucky bargain he had made.

"If I've only got a piece of bread with me, whenever I like I can eat butter and cheese with it; and when I'm thirsty I can drink milk. What could I possibly want more!"

On he walked and presently, when he came to an inn, he halted, ate up all his bread, and gave his last coppers for half a glass of beer. Then he drove his cow on further, towards his mother's village.

After a while he found himself on a wide heath that would take him more than an hour to cross. There wasn't a scrap of shade and he began to feel so hot and parched that his tongue stuck to the roof of his mouth.

"I can soon find a cure for this," thought Hans. "Now's the very time to milk my cow and quench my thirst." So he tied her to a bush and, as he had no pail, he held his leather cap to milk into; but try as he would, not a drop of milk could he get from her, for the fact was that Hans was no better at milking than he was at riding. While he was trying, he made the poor cow feel very uncomfortable and, at last, she couldn't bear it any more and gave him a kick on the head that knocked him down, so there he lay.

It wasn't long before a butcher came by, pushing a young pig in a wheelbarrow.

"What is the matter with you?" said the butcher as he helped Hans up.

Hans told him what had happened, and the butcher gave him a flask, saying:

"There, take a swig at this! That old cow will give you no milk! She's an old beast, good for nothing but the slaughter-house."

"Deary me!" said Hans, scratching his puzzled head. "Who would have thought it! If I kill her, she won't be much good to me. I hate cow-beef, it's not tender enough! If she were a young pig now! That really is tender and then there are the lovely sausages."

"Well," said the butcher, "just to please you, I'll change, and give you the pig for the cow."

"Heaven reward you for your kindness!" said Hans. So he gave the butcher the cow, took the pig out of the wheelbarrow, and drove it off, holding it by the string that was tied to one of its back legs.

Everything seemed to Hans to be all right now, as he jogged on again. He had met with some misfortunes to be sure; but he felt that he was now well repaid for it all.

The next person he met was a lad who was carrying a fine white goose under his arm, and when they had begun to chat, Hans told him how he had made so many good bargains. The lad, in his turn, told Hans that he was taking the goose to a christening.

"Feel!" said the lad, holding up the goose. "Feel how heavy she is! She's been fattened for the last eight weeks. Whoever roasts and eats her can cut plenty of fat off her!"

"You're right," said Hans, as he too held up the goose by her wings, "but my pig is no trifle."

Meantime the lad had begun to look grave and to shake his head.

"Hark'ee," said he, "I'm afraid that pig of yours may get you into trouble. In the village I've just come from, the Mayor had a pig that was marked very like that one. It's been stolen out of his sty. I was dreadfully afraid, directly I saw you, that it was the Mayor's pig you'd got. How do we know it isn't? If it is, it will be a bad job if they catch you; the least they'll do, will be to throw you into the horsepond."

Poor Hans was terribly worried to hear such news. "Goodness!" said he. "You know this country better than I—take my pig and give me the goose."

"Well, if I do," answered the lad, "I ought to have something into the bargain. However, I'll agree, as you're in trouble!" Then the lad took the string in his hand, and drove off the pig by a side path; while Hans, with the goose under his arm, went on his way free from care.

"After all," thought he, "I think I've got the best of the bargain; first there will be a capital roast; then the dripping will be enough to spread on my bread for six months; and then there are all the beautiful white feathers; I'll put them into a pillow, and then with such a fine pillow as that for my head, I'm sure I shall sleep soundly without rocking."

As he came to the very last village before he got to his own, Hans saw a scissors-grinder with his wheel, who was working away and singing these words:

"My scissors I grind and my wheel I turn
And all good fellows my trade should learn
For all that I meet with just serves my turn."

Hans stood still and watched him for a while, and at last he said:

"You seem to be well off, Mister Grinder! You seem so happy at your work!"

"Yes," said the scissors-grinder. "Mine's a golden trade; a good grinder never puts his hand in his pocket without finding money in it. But where in the world did you buy that beautiful fat goose?"

"I didn't buy it, but changed my pig for it."

"And where did you get the pig?"

"I gave a cow for it."

"And the cow?"

"I gave a horse for it."

"And the horse?"

"I gave a piece of gold as big as my head for that."

"And the gold?"

"Oh! That was my wages for seven long years."

"You've got on very well with all your bargains so far," said the grinder thoughtfully. "Now if you could only find money in your pocket whenever you put your hand into it, your fortune would be made!"

"Very true," answered Hans, "but how is that to be managed?"

"You must turn grinder like me," said the other. "You only need a grindstone; the rest will come of itself! Here's a stone that's almost new—very little the worse for wear really: I wouldn't ask more than the value of your goose for it. Will you buy?"

"How can you ask such a question?" replied Hans. "I should be the happiest man in the world, if I could have money whenever I put my hand in my pocket; what could I want more? There! Take the goose!"

"Now," said the grinder, as he gave Hans a common rough stone that lay by the path, "this is really a most capital stone! You can even straighten old bent nails by hammering them on it!"

Hans took the stone and went off with a light heart: his eyes sparkled for joy, and he said to himself, "I must have been born under a lucky star! Everything that I want or could possibly wish for, comes to me of itself."

Meantime he began to be tired, for after all he had

been travelling ever since daybreak; he was hungry, too, for he had eaten his bread long ago and spent his last coppers on half a glass of ale in his joy at getting the cow. At last he felt so weary that he could go no farther; for one thing carrying the stone tired him terribly. He dragged himself to the side of a pond so that he might drink some water and, as he lay down to drink, he set the stone carefully by his side on the bank; but the cool water tasted so good that Hans forgot all about the stone so that, by mistake, he pushed it a little. Down it rolled, *plump!* into the pond. Hans watched it sinking in the clear water. When it had really gone he sprang up, then fell upon his knees again for joy while he thanked Heaven with tears in his eyes for taking away his only plague, the ugly, heavy stone.

"How happy am I!" cried Hans. "No mortal was ever so lucky as I am."

Then up he got, and walked on, with a light and merry heart, free from all his troubles and was soon safe with his mother at home.

THE WOLF AND THE SEVEN
LITTLE KIDS

ONCE UPON A TIME THERE WAS A MOTHER GOAT
who had seven little kids whom she loved dearly.
One day she had to go out to get more food and, before
she started, she called the seven little kids to her. This is
what she said:

"Dear children! I've got to go to the forest for food.
Please keep the cottage door shut while I am away, and be
on your guard against the Wolf who will very likely try to
get in if he finds out that I am away. If he does get in, he
will eat you all up in a twinkling—hoofs, hide, hair and
all! Now listen carefully! The Wolf is very cunning and
he will try all sorts of tricks, but you can always know him
by two special signs. He has a *rough voice* and he has
black feet."

"We will take good care of ourselves," answered the
kids. "You need not worry at all, dear Mother. We have
understood everything."

The Mother Goat bleated tenderly to them, and
bending her head gave each of the seven kids a parting
kiss and then off she went.

The kids fastened the door safely behind her, and then
they began to make the house tidy. This was to be a
surprise for their mother. But they hadn't been busy

long before they heard a knocking at the door and then a voice called out:

"Open the door, dear children! Your mother is here."

But the voice did not sound at all like that of their mother, for it was rough and hoarse, so the kids didn't open the door, but instead they called out:

"No, no! You're not our mother! She has a soft, kind voice, but your voice is rough. You are the Wolf!"

Well, as you can guess, it really was the Wolf, so now, as the kids wouldn't open the door, he had to go away, and very angry he was. He gnashed his teeth and as soon as he was out of earshot he began to growl to himself, deep down in his throat.

Then he sat down and thought. Presently he got up and trotted off to the village where there was a shop and, managing to control his bad temper, he asked the shopman, quite politely, for some treacle. The shopman asked him how he would have it.

"In my mouth, if you please!" answered the Wolf, looking very sly.

Well, the shopman was a simple fellow and, though he was rather surprised, he did as the Wolf asked and poured the treacle right into the Wolf's big mouth, and all over his long red tongue.

Off trotted the Wolf again back to the cottage where the seven kids lived. Once more he knocked, "*Rat tat!*" and this time he called in a very sweet voice:

"Open the door, dear children, your mother is here, and she has brought you something nice to eat from the forest."

Well, the voice sounded all right, but it happened that there was a crack under the door and one of the kids stooped down, and what should she see but the Wolf's black feet as he stood there telling them that he was their mother.

"No, no," cried the kid who had spied the black feet, and all the others called out with her, "No, no! Our mother has got beautiful *white* feet but you have got black ones. You are the Wolf!"

Then the Wolf was more angry than ever.

Once more he gnashed his teeth and now the fur fairly bristled on his back, and again, as soon as he was out of hearing he growled deep down in his throat.

Now there was another shop in the village, a baker's shop. The Wolf went in and, putting on a very pitiful look, he began to limp.

"Oh, Baker," said the Wolf in his sweet treacly voice, "I have hurt my poor feet. Could you please rub some dough on them for me?"

Well, the baker was as simple as the shopkeeper and, though he was rather surprised, he did what the Wolf asked and put good dollops of soft dough on the Wolf's black feet.

This time the Wolf did not go straight back to the cottage; he went instead to the flour-mill.

"Miller," said the Wolf, once more speaking in his sweet treacly voice, "please will you dust some of your white flour over my feet."

Now the miller was not so simple as the other two and he thought to himself: "That Wolf wants to deceive someone." But aloud he said, "I haven't got any flour to spare for the like of you!"

But when he said that, the Wolf gnashed his terrible long teeth and began to growl deep down in his throat and said in quite a different voice:

"If you won't do it, I'll eat you!"

Then the miller was frightened, and did as he was asked and made the Wolf's paws white for him. (People are like that, you know.) So now, at last, the Wolf felt sure that his disguise was perfect and the wicked creature went, for the third time, to the door of the cottage. Then once more he knocked, *"Rat tat!"*

"Open the door, my dear, sweet, little children! Your loving mother has come from the forest and has brought something lovely for every one of you!"

The Wolf's white feet

This time the kids thought the voice sounded all right, and the one who had looked before really could see white feet under the crack of the door. So, what with the sweet voice, and what with the white feet, they thought it really must be their mother this time. They were in a great hurry to see what the lovely things were that had been brought them from the forest, so they unbolted and opened the door as quick as ever they could.

And there, in the open doorway, stood the wicked Wolf himself! You can imagine how frightened they were! But it was too late! The first kid was caught as he tried to

153

hide under the table, the second as she tried to get under the bed, the third as he tried to get under the washing-tub, the fourth as she bolted into the oven, the fifth as she tried to get into a cupboard, and the sixth as he tried to run out of the back door. One by one the Wolf gobbled them down, hoofs, hide, hair and all! Only one kid escaped, and that was the youngest and smallest. While the Wolf was swallowing down the others she managed to get inside the case of the big old grandfather clock, and the Wolf—who, luckily, wan't very good at counting—never even knew that he was *one kid short*!

When he had done eating, you can imagine how that Wolf licked his lips, and how fat he looked for he had had six whole kids for his dinner! He had eaten them, hoofs, hide, hair and all! He felt very sleepy too, so he took himself off and he laid himself down, and he went sound asleep under a tree in a green meadow not far from a beautiful well.

It wasn't long before the Mother Goat came home from the forest.

Ah! What a sight she saw! The house door stood wide open; the tables, chairs and benches were all thrown about, the washing-tub was on the floor, the blankets and pillows were pulled off the beds! She looked everywhere for her children, but she couldn't see one of them. Then she began to call them each by name beginning with the eldest. There was no answer.

But at last when she came to the name of the youngest, a soft voice said:

"Dear Mother, I'm in the clock case!"

Then the Mother Goat took the kid out, licked her and kissed her and begged her to tell all that had happened. When the little kid had told the sad tale, you can imagine how the poor Mother Goat cried and wept over the cruel fate of her six dear children!

At last, in her grief, she went out, and the youngest kid ran out with her. They walked on till, quite by chance, they came to the green meadow with a tree in it, and there, what should they see but the wicked Wolf himself, fast asleep, and snoring so loudly that the branches of the tree shook!

The smallest kid was very much frightened, but the Mother Goat came softly near, and when she was quite close, she could see that something was moving in the Wolf's fat swollen body.

"Ah, Heavens!" exclaimed the Mother Goat. "Can my children still be alive inside the wicked Wolf?" So she told the youngest kid to run quickly back to the cottage for scissors and a needle and thread, while she kept watch over the snoring Wolf.

Directly the kid was back, the Mother Goat took the scissors and, as fast as she could, *Snip! Snip!* she cut a long slit in the stretched skin of the Wolf's stomach. No sooner had she done this than a little kid popped out its head. She cut the hole a little bigger and then, out jumped the first kid alive and well. A moment after, all its five brothers and sisters followed, one after the other. The Wolf had been so greedy that he had swallowed them all down whole—hair and hide, hoofs, and all—so that they were not a bit the worse for their terrible adventure!

But there was no time yet for much rejoicing, for the Wolf might wake up, so, as soon as she had seen that they were all right, the Mother Goat in a great hurry sent each kid to look for a big stone. With these stones she filled the wicked creature's stomach and, as soon as this was done, sewed him up again. So quickly and quietly did she do all this, and so deeply was the Wolf sleeping, and so loudly was he snoring, that he never woke up at all.

When everything was finished, the Mother Goat and the kids went and hid where they could see what would happen next, and they hadn't long to wait, for the Wolf had nearly had his sleep out. So now he woke. First he yawned, then he stretched himself, and, at last, he tried to get on his legs again.

Now, as you can imagine, though the kids had been heavy, the stones were heavier still, and, as he stood up and tried to shake himself, the stones began to rattle in his stomach and this made him feel rather queer. He thought that perhaps he would feel better if he had a drink of water from the well, but, when he began to walk down to it, the stones rattled and knocked worse than ever. Then cried the Wolf:

> "What rumbles and tumbles
> Against my poor bones?
> I thought 'twas six kids
> But it feels like big stones!"

As he spoke he reached the well, and, as he stooped to drink, the weight of the stones overbalanced him. Into the water he fell. The water was deep and the stones weighed him down so that he sank at once and was drowned.

When the seven kids saw what had happened they all came running with their mother, and they made a circle round the well, dancing for joy and calling out:

"The Wolf is dead! The Wolf is dead!"

And then they and their mother lived happy ever after.

THE GREAT IRON CHEST

Long, long, ago, in the days when wishing was still some use, a King's son was put under a spell by a wicked old witch. As soon as he was quite in her power, she shut him up in a great iron chest. Then, by means of her magic, she set Prince, chest, and all, down in the middle of a lonely and enchanted forest.

No one in the whole wide world knew what had become of the Prince, and though the poor old King, his father, sent men far and wide to search for him, it was all of no use, and in fact, even if any of his men had been lucky enough to find the chest they could not have got the Prince out, for the spells that the witch had put on it had made it impossible for the like of them to set him free. Year after year the chest stood there in the great wild forest.

At last it happened that, in that very forest, a King's daughter lost her way, and, as she tried this way and that, she wandered into the most enchanted part. For nine whole days the poor Princess wandered in that great wild forest, and at last she saw before her something strange. Coming closer, she saw to her surprise that it was a great iron chest.

A voice spoke.

"Where do you come from and where are you going?"

"I am lost, and cannot get home to my father's kingdom," answered she.

The voice spoke again.

"I will help you, and you shall get home again safe and sound. But, if I give you this help, you must promise to do what I ask you. Do not fear! I am the son of a King who is much greater than your father. What I ask is your hand in marriage."

When she heard this, the Princess was afraid, and said to herself:

"Good heavens! What shall I do if it turns out that I have promised to marry a great iron chest?" But she had already wandered for nine days and was no nearer getting out of the forest than she had been at the beginning, so what could she do but promise?

Then the voice told her what she must do.

"You must come back alone to this spot—you will find it easily enough next time. With you, you must bring a knife, and with the knife you must scrape a hole in the side of the iron chest."

Well, the Princess said that she would do this, and as soon as she had given her word, a Companion stood beside her, whose face she could not see. This Companion walked near her, but did not speak, but in two hours the Princess was safe home again, and the Companion had vanished.

Great was the joy in her father's court when the lost Princess came home safe. The old King, her father, fell on her neck and kissed her. But the Princess was troubled and she said to him:

"Dear Father, I have suffered terribly! I wandered in the forest for nine days, but then, in the loneliest part of it, I found a great iron chest. When I came close a voice spoke to me. I don't know if it was the chest itself that spoke or something that was in the chest, but I had to give my word to the voice to go back alone, to set it free and then to marry it."

The old King was terrified when he heard of the promise that she had had to give, so terrified that he all but fainted. She was his only daughter and he loved her tenderly. At last he said that he could not bear that she should go. They would send the miller's daughter instead, for she was a very beautiful girl, and surely a great iron chest would never know the difference?

Now the miller's daughter, as well as being beautiful, was a bold girl, and was willing to try her luck, especially when she heard the voice had spoken of being the son of a King who was even more powerful than the Princess's father.

So off the miller's daughter set, with the knife with which she was to scrape a hole in the iron chest and she found the place easily enough. All that day, and far into the night, she scraped, but she could not stir the least chip off the iron! At last the night was ending and it began to grow light, and, from the chest, a voice said:

"It seems to me that it is nearly day outside?"

"Yes," said she, "it seems to me that I can hear the sound of my father's mill beginning to grind."

"So you are the miller's daughter!" said the voice. "Go your ways, and tell the Princess to come!"

So the girl went home, and away to the King, and she told him that the voice would have none of her, and that it had said it must have the King's daughter! But, once more, the poor old King could not agree to let the Princess go. So this time he gave the swineherd's daughter a piece of gold and a knife, and told her to try her luck. She too was a pretty girl and bold, and she also was quite willing. In her turn she found the chest and began to scrape, but not a flake of the iron could she stir, though she scraped away for dear life, and though she kept at it all that day and all the next night.

Once more, when day dawned, the voice said:

"It seems to me that it is nearly day outside?"

The girl answered yes, and that it seemed to her that she could hear her father blowing his horn to call the village pigs together, so that he could take them out to rout in the forest.

"So you are the swineherd's daughter?" answered the voice. "Go your ways and tell the King's daughter to come! Tell her that if she does not keep her word this third time, everything in her father's kingdom will fall into ruin, and not one stone will be left standing on another."

So the swineherd's daughter went back, just as the miller's daughter had done, and away to the King and the Princess to tell them what the voice had said.

When she heard what the girl had to tell, the Princess began to weep, but now it seemed that there was nothing for it—she would have to keep her promise. So she took a sad leave of her father, put a knife into her pocket and set out alone for the wild forest. It was easy to find the way, and when she got to the great iron chest, she began to sigh, but still she did scrape with her knife, just as the other girls had done. But this time the iron soon began to flake off so that when she had only worked for two hours, she had already scraped a small spy-hole right through the side. She peeped through it and there, inside, she saw a young man. She could see that he was handsome, that his hair shone like gold, and that he was splendidly dressed.

So now the Princess began to work away with a will, for, though many young men had courted her, she thought that she had never seen a suitor that she liked half as well as she liked the unknown Prince to whom, without knowing, she had made her promise. So, working hard, chipping and scraping, it wasn't so very long before she had made the hole big enough for him to get out. There he stood before her, and he was the handsomest young Prince that you could wish to see! He took her hand and said:

"Now you are mine and I am yours! You are my true bride because you have set me free!"

And with that he wanted to take her straight to his father's kingdom, but she begged him to let her go first to say farewell to her old father. The Prince looked uneasy. However, at last, he said she might go, but, added he:

"You must speak no more than three words to your father and then you must come back here again immediately."

Yes, the Princess agreed, she would do this.

— 2 —

But, oh dear! When she got home, without thinking, she spoke more than the three words to her old father, and (though she was not there to see) no sooner had she spoken the fourth word, than chest and Prince were transported far away over glass mountains and piercing swords.

So now, when she had taken leave of her father and when she came back to the place in the great wild forest where she ought to have found the iron chest and her handsome lover, they were nowhere to be seen.

The Princess began to call and search about, but all in vain. So now, once more, the poor girl wandered for nine days, always calling and seeking for some trace of her Prince. This time she had brought a little money, but not much, and a little food, but not much. So, by the evening of the ninth day, she was nearly dead with grief, disappointment, and hunger. Darkness came on, and then she did what she had done on each of these eight weary nights, she climbed into the branches of a tree so as to be safe from prowling beasts.

But this time, from her tree, she saw a small twinkling light. Climbing down again, she walked towards it, and as she went, she said her prayers. As she got nearer, she could see that the light came from the window of a little cottage, but the strange thing was that the path to the door was all overgrown with grass and brambles, as if no human footsteps ever came or went, but she also saw that a little heap of new-cut firewood lay near the door. She didn't much like the look of all this, so, before knocking, she peeped in through the window. What was her surprise to see, inside the cottage, a table beautifully spread with silver dishes with roast meat on them, and

with silver cups full of wine. But there wasn't a single human person to be seen, only a whole company of toads, some big and some quite little.

"Alas, whither have I come!" thought the poor Princess. However, after watching for a while, she took courage and knocked at the door. Then a big fat toad that she had already noticed, spoke to one of the others:

> "Little green waiting-maid,
>   Waiting-maid with the limping leg,
>   Little dog of the limping leg,
>   Hop hither and thither,
>   And quickly see who is outside."

At that a small toad came hopping along, and opened the door to her. When the Princess, who was rather frightened, stepped into the room, the toads welcomed her politely and told her to sit down and eat and drink. When she had finished they asked her:

"Where do you come from and where are you going?"

So then the Princess told them the whole story, of her promise and all the rest, and how now she could find neither Prince nor chest, though she had wandered for nine days in the great wild forest seeking and calling. Then the big old toad said:

> "Little green waiting-maid,
>   Waiting-maid with the limping leg,
>   Little dog of the limping leg,
>   Hop hither and thither,
>   And bring me the great box."

The same little toad hopped over to a corner and brought out the box. But it seemed that it wasn't to be opened yet. Instead, the toads led the Princess to a well-made bed which felt like silk and velvet, and she said her prayers and laid herself down on it and slept.

When morning came, the big old toad gave her certain gifts which she took out of the great box. They were three large needles, a plough-wheel, and three walnuts.

"Take care of these things for you will need them," said the toad. "You'll have to cross a high glass mountain, and go over three piercing swords, and then over a great lake, and then you will see a castle." The toad told her how to use the magic presents, and also whom she would find in the castle, and then added: "Do not open the nuts till you have done the things that I have already told you. Then, at last, if you can manage to do everything just as it should be done, you will get your lover back."

So, when the Princess had thanked the toads for all their kindness, she went on her way.

She went and she went, and a long and a weary way it was. At last she came to the glass mountain, and it was so slippery that she couldn't climb up. But when she found that she kept slipping back, she remembered to do exactly what the toad had told her. She stuck in one of the three needles, first behind one foot, and then another one before the next foot, pulling each needle out and putting it in again as she climbed. The needles made good footholds for her, and so, at last, she got over the glass mountain. Then she hid her needles in a place which she marked carefully.

After this she came to the three piercing swords, and these would have cut her to the bone, but they could not, because she rolled safely over them on her plough-wheel. When she was over this danger as well she hid the plough-wheel and, once more, she marked the place carefully. And now the great lake lay before her, but she knew that she must not use any of her magic gifts for this, but must wade and swim as best she could.

At last, when she had got over the water and over the

next hill, she saw before her a fine castle and, because of what the toad had told her, she knew that her Prince, whom she had set free from the great iron chest, was there.

She went to the back door and told the servant who opened it that she was a poor girl and would like to be hired, and she was taken on as a scullery-maid at low wages. Soon, as she worked, she found out from the talk of the other servants that the Prince was to be married to the lady of the castle.

"This is a new bride," they told her. "The maiden to whom he was first betrothed—the Princess who set him free from the iron chest—has been long dead, so now he is going to marry our lady."

She said nothing to that, but, in the evening, when she had washed up and done, she felt in her pocket for the three walnuts which the oldest toad had given her. She cracked one of them and, inside, what should she find but a royal dress which spread out without a crease as soon as she had shaken it free of the nut-shell.

The new bride soon heard about this strange and splendid dress, came down to the kitchen, had a look at it, and asked the Princess to sell it to her saying haughtily:

"That's not at all the right sort of dress for a servant-girl!"

But the Princess said "No!" She wouldn't sell it, but if the new bride would let her watch for one night in the room where the Prince lay, then she could have the beautiful dress for nothing.

The bride looked and looked at the dress, and thought that she had never seen anything so beautiful, and at last she agreed. When it was evening she said to her bride-groom:

"That silly girl wants to watch in your room tonight."

"If you are willing so am I!" said the Prince.

But before he went to bed the bride gave him a glass of wine in which she had secretly put a sleeping-draught, and he slept so soundly that, do as she would, the poor Princess could not wake him. She called and she called to him, but all in vain.

"I set you free," said she, "when you were in the iron chest in the great wild forest! I sought you for nine days! I climbed a glass mountain! I went over three sharp swords and a great lake before I found you, and now, though I am here by your side, you will not hear nor hearken!"

Now some of the servants slept nearby and, in the night, they could hear how somebody wept and pleaded the whole night through. But they said nothing.

On the second evening, when she had again washed up and done, the Princess cracked the second nut and, once more, the bride soon heard of a yet more splendid dress. She came down to the kitchen, and again they made the same bargain. But once more, the Princess could not wake the Prince because he had again been secretly given a sleeping-draught. But this time the servants were able to hear the words that she said:

"I set you free when you were in the iron chest in the great wild forest! I sought you for nine days! I climbed a glass mountain! I went over three sharp swords and a great lake before I found you, and now, though I am here by your side, you will not hear nor hearken!"

This time, when morning came, the servants came and told the Prince of the strange words that they had heard in the night.

Then came the third evening and, when she had washed

167

up and done, the Princess cracked the third walnut. This third dress was the most splendid of all, for it was not only of the finest silk like the others, but was stiff with pure gold. The false bride wanted this dress even more than she had wanted the others and, since she had been so successful with the sleeping-draught, she was very glad to make the very same bargain.

But the Prince had guessed that it had been because of the wine that he had slept so soundly on the other two nights, so, this time, though he pretended to drink it, he managed to pour it all away without being seen. However, he lay down on his bed as usual, and when the Princess came to watch by him, he seemed to her to be as fast asleep as on the other nights.

This made the Princess very sad, for now she had

" Though I am here you will not hear nor hearken "

nothing more with which to bargain with the false bride, so this was the last time she would be able to come to him.

"Dearest love," said she, as she bent over him, "I set you free when you were in the iron chest in the great wild forest! I sought you for nine days! I climbed a glass mountain! I went over three sharp swords and a great lake before I found you, and now, though I am here by your side, you will not hear nor hearken!"

Scarcely had she spoken when the Prince sprang up joyfully and, giving her his hand, he said:

"You are the true bride! You are mine and I am yours! Just as we vowed in the great wild forest!"

Then they embraced each other in great happiness.

But this was not the Prince's own castle, but an enchanted place that belonged to the false bride, so they resolved to steal away while it was still dark, and before they left they took away all the false bride's clothes so that she would be slow to follow them. Then off they bowled in a carriage to which the swiftest horses in the stable were harnessed. When they came to the great lake there was a boat ready for them. When they came to the piercing swords, the Princess pulled out the plough-wheel from where she had hidden it. When they got to the glass mountain she brought the three great needles out of their hiding-place.

And so, at last, they made their way back—all that long journey. And they found that they were back in the enchanted part of the great wild forest, the place where all their adventures had begun. But now they found that everything there had changed. Meadows full of flowers and orchards of fruit-trees smiled where once the wild dark tangle of trees had shut out the sky. Then they went, hand in hand, to try to find the place where the little old house had once stood. But that had changed too, and so had the good toads, for the little old house had become a splendid castle, and the toads were all disenchanted and had their own shapes again, and were King's children.

It was in this splendid castle that the wedding-feast was held. The Princess's old father came to the feast and was overjoyed to see his dear daughter safe and sound. But when the feasting was over and when it was time to say good-bye he seemed so sad and lonely that they could not bear to part with him so they invited him to stay on and live with them.

So now the Prince and the Princess had two kingdoms between them, and they ruled long and happily over them both.

A mouse did run;
The tale is done.

THE ELVES AND THE SHOEMAKER

Once upon a time a young shoemaker lived in a cottage by the side of the road. Times were bad and got worse so that he and his wife became so poor that, at last, she had only one loaf in the cupboard and he had nothing left but the leather to make one pair of shoes. A very sad fix as you will agree! However, the young man cut out the shoes and laid them on his work-bench ready to sew next morning. There was, as you know, only one loaf left in the house, so when they had eaten part of it and had drunk some water, he and his wife quietly went to bed.

Next morning, when he looked at his work-bench, what was the shoemaker's surprise to see, not just cut-out leather, but a pair of shoes, very neatly made, standing quite ready. He took up the left shoe, and he took up the right shoe. He looked at the soles, and he looked at the uppers. There wasn't a stitch wrong! Both shoes were as neat and well-made as could be.

And now it seemed his luck was in, for soon afterwards, a customer came in, and the shoes were so nicely made, and fitted him so well, that he willingly paid a good price for them. So now, with the money, the shoemaker was able to buy, not only food for himself and his wife, but enough leather to make two pairs of shoes.

It was late when he got back with the leather, but after supper he sat down directly and cut it out so as to have the two pairs ready to sew in the morning, and then he and his wife went to bed and slept soundly. Next day he got up early so as to begin to stitch the shoes, but there was no need! To his surprise, there lay not one, but two pairs of shoes, just as well and neatly made as the first had been. This time two buyers came in, and now the shoe-maker not only had money for food for himself and his wife but, this time, to buy enough leather for four pairs of shoes.

Every day the same sort of thing happened. The shoe-maker would go and buy leather, cut out shoes from it overnight and, however many pairs he cut out, there they were, all stitched, nailed, and nicely finished by the next morning.

One evening, not long before Christmas, as they sat by the fire, the shoemaker said to his wife:

"Do you think we had better keep awake and watch tonight? It's really time we found out who it is that has been helping us."

His wife agreed and so they left a candle alight, and instead of drawing the bed-curtains and going to sleep, they left the curtains only half drawn and peered out between them to see what they would see.

For a while they saw nothing. Time passed. They watched and they watched. Still nothing happened, but at last, at midnight, the door of the house opened and two pretty little men ran quickly in. They were no bigger than three-year-old children and neither of them had so much as a rag to cover him. Down the pair of them sat to the shoemaker's work-bench, had a look at the work that was ready cut out, and then, in a moment, they began to stitch, sew and hammer. They worked so quickly and skilfully that the shoemaker was amazed, and couldn't take his eyes off them. The two little creatures worked so fast that it seemed to him that they hardly stopped to draw breath. Directly the work was done, and as soon as it all stood finished upon the work-bench, they both scampered away as quickly as they had come.

"Well," said the shoemaker's wife as soon as she and her husband were alone again, "these two little men have made us rich! Poor little things, running about so busily on a winter's night and with nothing on! They must be cold! I think we ought to show that we are grateful."

"Very true!" answered her husband.

"I'll tell you what I'll do!" said his wife. "I'll make them each a little shirt, I'll make two little coats, two waistcoats and two pairs of trousers. Then I'll knit them each a little pair of stockings, and your part will be to make them two small pairs of shoes!"

The shoemaker, who was as grateful as his wife, quite agreed to this plan. So, for a day or so, they were both busy, as you can guess. There was a lot for the wife to do and for the shoemaker too, for he wanted to make the shoes as pretty as ever he could. The end of it was that it was Christmas Eve before both clothes and shoes were all finished. But now, at last, when everything was ready, they laid out their presents, some on chairs and with the little shoes on the work-bench instead of the usual cut-out leather. Then once more they waited, well hidden behind the bed-curtains, very much hoping that their good, industrious little helpers would be pleased with the presents.

Again they had to wait until midnight, and then, once

more the door opened and the two little creatures came bouncing in. But now the little men looked around them bewildered! Where was the cut-out leather? But soon, of course, they saw what was meant by what was on the chairs and on the work-bench—the two small suits, the two pairs of warm stockings, the little white shirts and the pretty little pairs of shoes. They guessed at once that all these things were for them and you never saw two little creatures so delighted. They didn't wait a moment, but began to dress themselves directly, all the time hopping about and admiring each other and singing at the tops of their shrill little voices:

"Now we're boys so fine to see,
Why should we longer Cobblers be?"

Over and over they sang this song. Up on to the bench and over it they hopped and skipped, laughing away. Round and round the room they chased each other in fun. At last they opened the door and danced away, out into the moonlight.

From that time forward the shoemaker and his wife never saw the two little men again. But, though they never saw them, everything went well in that house from that time forward, so that the shoemaker and his wife lived happily ever after.

HANSEL AND GRETTEL

HANSEL AND GRETTEL WERE A WOODCUTTER'S
children. It was in a time when there was a famine all
over the country. Crops failed and things got so bad that
no one had money to buy wood, so that woodcutters had
no money to buy food.

"What is to become of us?" whispered the woodcutter
to his wife one night when they were alone. "How are
we to feed those two poor children?"

"We have only got one loaf left," said their stepmother in a low voice.

"What can we do?" answered their father in despair.

"If we all four die of hunger," answered she, "it won't
mend matters! I'll tell you what I suggest. Tomorrow
morning we will take the children out, quite early, into the
thickest part of the forest. We will light a fire and give
each of them a piece of this last loaf. Then we will go to
our work and leave them alone. They will not be able
to find their way back and perhaps as they wander, they
may have the good luck to find someone who can look
after them better than we can."

"No, wife," said the man, "we can't do that! I couldn't
find it in my heart to do it!"

"What a fool you are," said she. "It's the best chance

175

for all four of us. It is either that, or sawing the wood for our coffins at once."

Well, they whispered on for a while, the man very unwilling, the stepmother saying that it was the best chance for all of them.

Now the two children had not been able to sleep for hunger and had had heard what their stepmother and father had said.

Grettel wept bitterly and said, "It's all over with us now."

"Go to sleep, little sister," said Hansel. "Don't cry! I'll find some way out of it."

When the old people had gone to sleep, Hansel got up, put on his little coat, opened the door, and slipped out. The moon was shining brightly and some white pebbles, which lay scattered round the house, shone like newly-minted silver coins. Hansel stooped down and put as many into his pockets as they would hold. Then he went back and said to Grettel:

"Take comfort, little sister, and go to sleep. God won't forsake us."

And then Hansel went to bed again.

At daybreak, before the sun had quite risen, the woman came and said:

"Get up, you lazybones! We are going into the forest to fetch wood." Then she gave them each a piece of bread and said: "Here is something for your dinner, but don't eat it before then, for you'll get no more."

Grettel put the bread under her apron, for she knew that Hansel had got all those pebbles in his pockets. Then they all started for the forest. When they had gone a little way, Hansel stopped and looked back at the cottage, and he did the same thing again and again.

His father said:

"Hansel, what are you stopping to look back at? Hurry up! Put your best foot foremost."

"Oh, father," said Hansel, "I'm only looking at my white cat. It's sitting on the roof, wanting to say good-bye to me."

"Little fool, that's no cat! It's the morning sun shining on the chimney," said the stepmother.

But Hansel had not been looking for the cat. He had dropped a white pebble on the ground each time he stopped.

When they got deep into the forest, their father said: "Now, children, pick up some fallen wood. I want to make a fire to warm you."

Hansel and Grettel gathered twigs and branches together and soon made a big pile. Then the pile was lighted, and, when it blazed up the woman said:

"Now lie down by the fire and rest yourselves while we go and cut wood. When we have finished we will come back to fetch you."

Hansel and Grettel sat by the fire, and when dinner-time came they each ate their little bit of bread, and they thought their father was quite near because they could hear the sound of an axe. It wasn't the axe, however, but a branch, which the man had tied to a dead tree and which blew backwards and forwards against it. They sat there for a very long time and, after a while, they both felt tired. Then their eyes began to close and they were soon fast asleep. When they woke the fire was out and it was dark night.

Grettel began to cry and to ask: "How shall we ever get out of the wood?"

But Hansel comforted her and said:

"Wait a little while, wait till the moon rises, and then we shall find our way."

When the moon rose, Hansel took his little sister's hand and they began to walk back, guided by the pebbles, which glittered in the moonlight like newly coined silver money. They walked the whole of the rest of the night, and, at daybreak, they found themselves back at their father's cottage.

They knocked at the door, and when their stepmother opened it and saw Hansel and Grettel she said:

"You bad children, why did you sleep so long in the forest? We thought you didn't mean to come back any more."

But their father was delighted, for it had gone to his heart to leave them behind alone, and, besides that, he had by good luck at last managed to sell a load of wood, and so they had got a little food again.

But it turned out that this was only just one bit of luck; things were not really any better. The famine was still going on. Another week went by, the food was eaten, and not another fire-log could he sell.

"We have eaten up everything again except half a loaf," said the woman to her husband, when she thought the children could not hear. "We must do the same thing again, but take them further this time. There is nothing else to be done."

"Oh, don't let us do that," said the man. "We had better share our last bit of bread with the children."

Well, the man had given in the first time and when she wouldn't agree he gave in now, and, just as Hansel and Grettel had been awake the first time, and had heard what passed, so it was again. Hansel thought that he would do the same thing with the pebbles, but oh, dear!

178

When he tried to get out the door was locked! Once more he tried to console his little sister.

"Don't cry, little sister, God will help us."

In the early morning the woman made the children get up, and she gave them each a piece of bread, but it was smaller than the last. On the way to the forest Hansel crumbled it up in his pocket, and stopped every now and then to throw a crumb or two on to the ground.

"Hansel, why do you keep stopping to look about you?" asked his father.

"I am looking at my dove which is sitting on the roof and wants to say good-bye to me," answered Hansel.

"Little fool," said the woman, "that's no dove! It's only the morning sun, shining on the chimney."

Nevertheless, Hansel went on strewing a crumb or two from time to time. The woman led the children deep into the forest, to a part where they had never been before. Again they made a big fire, and again she said:

"Stay where you are, children, and when you are tired you may go to sleep for a while. We are going farther on to cut wood. In the evening when we've finished we will come back and fetch you."

At dinner-time Grettel shared her bread with Hansel, for he had crumbled his to mark their way back. Then they went to sleep and the evening passed, but no one came to fetch the two children.

Once more it was quite dark when they woke up, and Hansel cheered his little sister. He said:

"Wait a bit, Grettel, till the moon rises, and then we can see the bread-crumbs which I scattered to show us the way home."

When the moon rose they started, but they found no bread-crumbs, for thousands of birds lived in the forest and they had picked them up and eaten them.

Morning came, but now they were lost indeed! Luckily it was the end of the summer, when there are always wild berries in the forest, but, believe me, it's hungry work to try to live on berries. Farther and farther they wandered. At last evening came once more and they lay down under a tree and went to sleep.

Hansel tries to mark the way

In the morning they were hungrier than ever. They felt quite weak with having so little to eat, but all the same they began to walk again and, once more, all they could find were a few berries and water from the streams.

About mid-day what should they see but a beautiful

bird, the like of which they had never seen before. It had perched on a bough, close to them, and there it sang so sweetly that the children stood for a long while, hand in hand, listening to it. Presently it spread its wings and flew a little way off and, as they thought it might settle and sing again, they followed. So now for a mile and more the bird sang and flew, and flew and sang among the trees and the children followed. At last it seemed to them that, as well as the bird, they could see something else gleaming through the green of the forest. Running quickly to see what it could be, they saw that the bird had perched on the roof of a little cottage.

— 2 —

But what a cottage! The whole thing—roof, walls chimneys and all—looked as if it was made of bread or else of cake. The hungry children came closer and saw that it really was so, and also that the window-panes were not made of glass but of sheets of clear sugar.

"I will eat a piece of the roof," cried Hansel, "and you can eat some window."

No sooner said than done. Hansel reached up and broke a piece off the cake roof, while Grettel stepped up to one of the little window-panes, broke off a corner and began to bite it. Then, as they ate, they heard a voice.

"Tip-tap, tip-tap, who raps at my door?"

But the half-starved children only left off eating long enough to answer:

"The wind, the wind, the child of heaven!" and went on munching.

The roof tasted so nice that Hansel tore off a great piece; while Grettel broke quite a large round pane

181

out of the window, and sat down to enjoy it better.

Then the door of the cottage opened, and a very old woman came out, walking with two sticks. Hansel and Grettel were so frightened that they let fall what they had in their hands; but the old woman, nodding her head, only said:

"Ah, you dear children, what has brought you here? Come in and stop with me, and no harm shall befall you." So saying she led them into her cottage. They saw that a good meal—milk and pancakes with sugar, apples and nuts—was already spread out on the table. The old woman sat them down and as they ate, the children saw that, in the back room, were two nice little beds, covered with white counterpanes. Here, when they could eat no more, Hansel and Grettel laid themselves down to sleep and thought themselves in Heaven.

Now the old woman, though at first she behaved so kindly, was really a wicked witch who waylaid boys and girls. She had built the bread-and-cake cottage on purpose to entice children, but as soon as she had got them into her power she used to kill, cook, and eat them. She was very greedy, and so when she managed to do this, it was a rare treat to her.

Early next morning, before Hansel and Grettel woke, the old witch hobbled up to have another look at them. There they lay peacefully sleeping after all their adventures.

"They want fattening," mumbled the old witch to herself. "But the boy will soon make a good bite!"

Then she pulled Hansel out of the bed with her rough hands and, without another word, she carried him off and shut him up in a little cage near the back door. Poor Hansel shouted out, but it was no use.

Then the old witch went back to Grettel and, shaking her till she woke, she said:

"Get up, you lazy thing, and fetch some water to cook something good for your brother. I'm going to keep him in that cage till he gets fat, and when he's fat enough I shall eat him."

Hansel pretends to stretch out his finger

Poor Grettel began to cry, but her tears were as useless as Hansel's shouts, for the old witch was able to make her do as she wished. So a nice meal was cooked for Hansel, but Grettel got nothing but a crab's claw.

Every morning, the old witch came to the cage and said:

"Hansel, stretch out your finger so that I can feel whether you are getting fat."

But every time when she said this, Hansel would stretch out a bone that he had saved from his last meal, and the old woman, who had very bad eyesight, thought it was his finger.

Time went on, and the witch began to wonder very much why Hansel was so slow about getting fat. When four weeks had passed, and it seemed to her that Hansel still kept quite lean, she lost patience, and decided not to wait any longer.

"Grettel," she called out in a passion, "get some water quickly; be Hansel fat or lean, this morning I mean to kill and cook him!"

Oh, how the poor little sister grieved as she was forced to fetch the water, and how fast the tears ran down her cheeks!

"Dear good God, help us now!" she exclaimed. "If we had been eaten by the wild beasts in the wood, at least we should have died together."

The old witch heard her crying and called out:

"Leave off that noise! It won't help you a bit!"

So now Grettel made a fire and filled the big iron pot and put it on to boil.

"First, we will bake, however," said the witch, "I've already heated the oven, and kneaded the dough," and with that she pushed poor Grettel up to the other fire which the witch herself had lighted under the big bread oven. The flames had begun to burn fiercely. "Creep into the oven," said the witch, "and see if it is hot enough, and, if it is, we will put in the bread." What she really meant to do, as soon as Grettel got in, was to shut the oven door on her and let her bake, so that she might eat her as well as Hansel.

But Grettel guessed what her thoughts were, and said: "I don't know how to do it; how shall I get in?"

"You stupid goose!" said the witch. "The door is plenty big enough! See, I could even get in myself!" So saying she stooped and put her own head into the oven. Grettel quickly gave her a hard push from the back and in the witch went, headlong, so that, in a trice, Grettel was able to shut the oven door, and when it was shut she bolted it. Oh, how horribly the old witch howled! But Grettel didn't wait to listen, she ran to Hansel and, opening the door, called out:

"Hansel, we're saved; the old witch is in the oven!"

Out Hansel sprang like a bird when its cage is opened. They were so glad to be safe that they fell upon each other's necks, and kissed each other over and over again. Now at last there was nothing to fear. So they went all over the witch's house, and, in every corner, as well as plenty of stored food, there were chests and barrels full of pearls and precious stones.

"These pearls and diamonds are better than those white pebbles," said Hansel, putting as many into his pocket as it would hold; while Grettel, thinking that she would take a few as well, filled her apron.

"We had better be off now," said Hansel, "and get out of this enchanted forest as quickly as we can."

So off the two went. But when they had walked for about two hours they came to a large piece of water. "How can we get over it?" said Hansel. "I can see no bridge at all."

"And there is no boat either," said Grettel. "But look!

Over yonder there swims a white duck; I will ask her to help us over;" so Grettel sang:

> "Little Duck, good little Duck,
>   Grettel and Hansel, here we stand;
> There is neither stile nor bridge,
>   Take us on your back to land."

No sooner had she done singing than the duck came to them, and Hansel sat himself on her back and told his sister to come and sit behind him.

"No," answered Grettel. "We shall be too many for the good little duck; she shall take us over one at a time." This the good little bird did and, when both were safely on the other side and had gone a little way, they found that they had got to a place that they knew quite well. So, at last, they saw their father's cottage. Then they began to run, and bursting into the house, they fell on their father's neck.

He had not had one happy hour since the children had been left in the forest; and as for their stepmother, she had died. Grettel shook her apron so that the pearls and precious stones rolled out upon the floor, while Hansel fished one handful of treasure after the other out of his pockets. Then all their sorrows were ended, and they lived together in great happiness.

THE WORLD UPSIDE DOWN,
OR SCHLAURAFFEN-LAND

———— ❧❦❧ ————

"SCHLAURAFFEN-LAND?" "THE WORLD UPSIDE DOWN?"
Is that a place or is it a time? Decide for yourself! Anyhow
I was there, and I can tell you a great deal about it.

How to find it? To start with you have to go three
miles behind Christmas. Is that clear?

When you get there, you come to two towns where the
walls of the houses are all made of gingerbread, the
rafters are made of roast pork, and the roofs are cakes. In
the country-part that lies round about this town, the
hedges are made of sausages. When it rains, it doesn't rain
water, but milk and cream, and if it hails and you pick up
the hailstones, you find they are sweets. Grown-up people
are paid for playing and rewarded for sleeping, but nobody ever says anything about giving anybody money for
working, or giving prizes to children for doing their
lessons. It's only for playing about that prizes are given.

One of the first things I saw while I was on my way
there, was the City of Rome. The whole town was
hanging by a small silken thread, and close to the road
to it I saw an old man, without feet, who could run faster
than a racehorse. Oh! Yes! I nearly forgot to tell you that
I also saw a handsome donkey who had a silver nose. This
donkey was running after two hares, and it chased them

187

under a great big lime tree on which grew very good hot cakes. Roast chickens kept flying about and I noticed that a crab was chasing another hare at full speed.

Have I told you enough lies? No? All right then! I saw a plough ploughing without being drawn either by an ox or a horse, and a child a year old who threw four huge mill-stones all the way from one town to another. Indeed he threw them from Ratisbon to Treves and then on from Treves to Strasbourg. I also saw a hawk which swam over the broad river Rhine (which he had a perfect right to do). In the water, as well as the hawk, there were two fish. These noisy creatures were quarrelling, shouting and making such a hullabaloo that the din could be heard for miles.

In the part of the country that I came to next there seemed to be some rather unusual creatures. For instance, there were two crows busy mowing a meadow, two gnats building a bridge, two doves tearing a wolf to pieces, and two mice busy making an ordinary priest into a bishop. Then, as I went on farther, a snail rushed past me, and with my own eyes I saw this snail kill two furious lions. As for the barber, he was so busy shaving off a woman's beard that he took no notice either of the snail or the lions.

Two greyhounds seemed to be as busy as the barber. They were bringing a whole water-mill up out of the river. I am glad to tell you that a wise old horse was looking on and he said that the greyhounds were doing quite right. Not far off, four other horses were threshing corn with all their might, two goats heated the stove, while a red cow stood by, ready to shoot the bread into the oven with her bread shovel. Just at that moment a cock crowed!

> "Cock-a-doodle-dôo!
> The story is all told!
> Cock-a-doodle-doo!"

JORINDA AND JORINGEL

———— ❀❀❀ ————

THERE WAS ONCE, IN THE VERY OLD TIME, A strange-looking, half-ruined castle that stood in the middle of a great wood, and in this castle there lived an old witch. At twilight she flew about in the form of an owl, in the day she crept about the country like a cat; but at night she always became an old woman again. When any young man came within a hundred paces of her castle, he had to stand still and couldn't move a step till she set him free. But when any pretty maiden came within that distance, she was never set free but was changed into a bird; and then the old witch would put her into a wicker-work cage and hang the cage up in one of the great rooms in the castle. There were seven thousand cages hanging there, each with a beautiful bird in it—wrens, doves, blackbirds, nightingales, warblers, and thrushes—all the birds you can think of.

Now in a neighbouring village there lived a maiden whose name was Jorinda. She was prettier than all the pretty girls that had ever been seen in those parts; and there was also a young man whose name was Joringel who was very fond of her, and the pair of them were betrothed and were soon to be married.

One day they went for a walk together, and Joringel said:

"We must take care that we don't go near to the castle!"

It was a beautiful evening; the last rays of the setting sun shone among the long trunks of the trees. Thrushes and blackbirds were singing and turtle-doves cooed among the fresh green of the young leaves.

Jorinda sat down to enjoy the lovely evening and Joringel sat by her side. But lovely though it was, they both felt sad, they did not know why; somehow they felt as if they were, somehow, going to be parted from one another. They had wandered far; and, when they saw that the sun would soon set behind the mountains, they began to think of going home. But now they were not quite sure where they had got to or what path to take.

Joringel got up from where they had been sitting and began to look about to find the way and it was then that, to his horror, he saw that, without knowing it, they were near the old castle. While he had been thus searching about, Jorinda had still sat there, and as she sat she sang:

> "My little bird, with the necklace red,
>   Sings sorrow, sorrow, sorrow,
>   He sings that the dove must soon be dead,
>   Sing sorrow, sor——*jug, jug, jug*."

The song stopped suddenly! Joringel turned to find out the reason, and saw that his dear Jorinda had been changed into a nightingale! Then he saw how an owl with fiery eyes flew three times round her and heard how three times the owl screamed:

> "Tu whit, Tu whoo! Tu whoo, Tu whoo!"

Joringel found that he could not move! He had to stand quite still and could neither weep nor speak, nor move hand nor foot. And now the sun went down altogether. The owl flew into a bush, and a moment after, out from behind that very bush there hobbled out a bent old woman—sallow and lean. She was muttering to herself, and then, suddenly putting out her hand, she caught the poor nightingale which seemed as little able to move as Joringel. As soon as she had got the bird, she went off with it in her hand towards the castle.

Poor Joringel saw well enough that his dear nightingale was gone—but what could he do? He could not speak, he could not move from the spot where he stood. It got quite dark. Then the moon rose. At last by its light he saw the witch come back. Then she sang in a hoarse voice:

> "Till the prisoner's fast,
> And her doom is cast,
>   There stay! Oh, stay!
> When the charm is around her,
> And the spell has bound her,
>   Hie away, away!"

A moment after, Joringel found himself free. Then he fell on his knees before the witch, and begged her to give him back his dear Jorinda. But the old woman only shook her head, told him that he should never see his darling again, and went her way.

Joringel could not bear to go back to his own home, so he went to a strange village and there he got a job at his own trade—he was a shepherd. Many a time he would drive his flock back to near the great wood, and long would he gaze at the strange old castle in the distance. He would walk round and round, coming as near as ever he dared.

At last one night he dreamt a dream. He dreamt that he found a beautiful blood-red flower, in the middle of which lay a great pearl. He dreamt that he picked the flower, and went with it in his hand into the castle, and that there everything he touched with it was freed from enchantment.

In the morning, when he awoke, he gave his flock to the care of another shepherd and he himself began to search over hill and dale to see if he could anywhere find a flower like the one he had held in his dream. Eight long days he searched in vain; but on the ninth day, early in the

" *You shall never see her again* "

morning, he found a blood-red flower, and in the middle of it was a large dewdrop as big as a splendid pearl.

Then he took the flower, and with it in his hand he went straight off to the castle. This time he found that he was not held fast, but could go close.

Joringel went on boldly, till at last, he touched the great gate with the flower. It immediately sprang open. Then he went on through the courtyard and through another door and came to a great room and here he saw the witch who was busy feeding the birds in the seven thousand cages.

When she turned and saw Joringel the witch was angry, very angry, and she scolded and spat poison at him, but because of the flower she could not come within two paces of him. He did not take any notice of her, but went and looked closely at the cages with all the many kinds of birds; but among them there were more than a hundred nightingales, so how was he to find his dear Jorinda again?

Just then he saw the old woman go quietly up to one cage, take it down and begin to shuffle off towards the door.

Swiftly he sprang towards her, and managed to touch the bird with the flower. In a moment his dear Jorinda stood before him in her true shape and as beautiful as ever! Then, with his magic flower, Joringel touched all the other birds whom the witch had changed and each one turned to her true shape again.

Jorinda and Joringel had the most beautiful wedding ever seen, for all the grateful girls who had once been birds came to it. They came from far and near in their best dresses, and they all looked so pretty and sang so sweetly and wished Jorinda and Joringel so much happiness that it was a joy to hear and to see.

SHIVER AND SHAKE

———— ❧ ————

LONG, LONG AGO, THERE LIVED TWO BROTHERS. Their father always said what a sharp sensible lad the ⌐ ¹er one was. As for the younger brother, whose name was Fritz, the father treated him as if he were nothing more or less than a Silly.

Now though the elder brother really was a sharp, sensible fellow, there was just one thing that, even when he was quite grown up, the elder brother didn't like. He didn't like going through the churchyard after dark and, if his father wanted him to go out and fetch something, he would always somehow manage to put off going that way until the next morning.

"Going through that churchyard in the dark makes me shiver and shake with fear!" he would say.

The younger son—the one that everyone called Silly— used to sit in the corner listening to his brother when he said this, and he couldn't think what in the world he meant.

"Other people are always saying that sort of thing—it makes me shiver and shake with fear," he would say to himself. "But I don't know anything about shivering and shaking with fear. What can they mean? It's time I learned! What a lot there is that I don't know!"

After a while it was time for the two lads to go out and seek their fortune. The elder son had learned a trade, so that was all right, but Fritz didn't know any trade, so his father asked him what he would like to learn.

"I should like to learn how to shiver and shake—I don't know how to do that at all!" said Fritz.

When his father and elder brother heard that, how they laughed!

"You'll learn soon enough, Silly!" said his father, still laughing and, with that, he gave each of them as much money as he could spare to start them off with.

After they had walked for a while their ways parted, for Fritz stuck to it that all he wanted to learn was just this one thing!

"Good luck to you then, Silly! You'll learn that fast enough!" said the elder brother. They shook hands and then each went his way.

Well, after he had journeyed alone for a time, Fritz met a waggoner who was going with his horse and cart to the next town. He went along with him and, as they went, they began to talk and the lad told the waggoner what it was that he wanted to learn.

"Well, you're a Silly indeed!" said the waggoner, laughing. "Never mind, you're a nice lad and I dare say we can find a job for you when we get to the town."

In the evening they came to an inn and the waggoner put his cart in the yard and his horse in the stable, and he and Fritz went to the inn kitchen. While they were sitting by the fire, the waggoner told the innkeeper, as a good joke, what it was that Fritz wanted to learn. At that the innkeeper laughed just as loud as his father and brother, and just as merrily as the waggoner.

"If that is all you want, you funny fellow," said

195

the innkeeper, "it'll be easy enough in this town!"

"Oh, husband!" said the innkeeper's wife, who was a kind woman. "Don't tell the lad about that! Too many nice young men have come to grief over it already—it would be a pity if such a good-natured lad as this should lose his life as well as the rest."

So then of course Fritz wanted to know all about it, and he would let the innkeeper have no peace. So at last the innkeeper said:

"Not far from here there stands an enchanted castle with a great treasure hidden in it. Whoever can manage to stay three nights in it, all alone, will be able to break the evil spell, and the King has promised that whoever can do this shall have his daughter in marriage and half his kingdom. This Princess is the most beautiful maiden that the sun ever shone on. But alas, the castle is guarded by evil spirits, and though many bold young men have tried to stay alone there for three nights, it has always been too much for them. Not one has ever come out alive."

The kind innkeeper's wife would hardly let him finish, but kept telling Fritz that he must not try, but that, instead, they would give him a job helping at the inn. But say what she might it was all no use. Fritz had made up his mind.

So the very next morning off he set for the palace and when he got there he asked to see the King. When he stood before him, Fritz at once asked if he could be the next to try to stay the three nights at the enchanted castle. The King looked at him sadly for, like the innkeeper's wife, he thought it was a pity that such a nice-looking lad should die like the others. So he only shook his head and told Fritz that he had better be off, for he would be sure to die of fright like the rest of them. But the lad begged him, saying that he really must be allowed to try.

"Do let me, your Majesty! There's nothing I want so much in the world as to learn how to shiver and shake with fright." At last he begged so hard that the King said:

"Have it your way then!" and then told him the conditions. "You may ask for three things to take into the castle with you," said the King, "but they mustn't, any of them, be alive, for you have to watch there quite alone. What will you take?"

Fritz thought for a while, then he said:

"First, I'll have plenty of firewood and something to kindle it with; second, food and drink; and third, a good strong carving-knife."

So the King agreed that these things could count as three, and ordered his men to bring them to the castle during the day. Then the lad went back to the inn, well pleased, and as he walked, he whistled, and he spent the rest of the day in helping the innkeeper's wife to wash the pots and beer-mugs.

When it began to grow dark, off he went alone to the enchanted castle. He made himself a good warm fire in one of the huge rooms, found a bench, drew it up to the fire, and sat himself down to wait for what would happen. For a while nothing happened at all. But towards midnight something began to cry miserably from one of the corners.

"Miau! Miau! How cold we are!"

"Don't be silly," called out Fritz, "if you're cold, come here and sit by the fire, and warm yourselves."

No sooner had he spoken than two black cats, as big as wolves, that looked at him savagely with their fiery eyes,

197

sprang out of two dark corners and sat down by the fire.
No sooner had these fierce cats sat down than, out of
every dark place in the huge room, more enormous black
cats began to creep out, and soon there were black dogs as
well. They all had eyes like coals and the dogs had red-
hot chains. More and more of them came, until the room

—big as it was—was crowded with them and they all miaued and barked and spat and growled and made a horrible noise. The lad didn't mind all that a bit. But soon the beasts began to paw at the fire and to pull it to pieces—this nearly put it out—so that the room began to get much darker. Then Fritz got cross and, standing up and taking up the big carving-knife, he called out: "Away with you!"

But instead of going away they began to snap and claw at him, and so then he began to slash at them. At that, some of them ran away with their tails between their legs, but the others he killed, and, opening a window, he threw their bodies, plop, down into the castle moat. When he had cleared up he made up the fire again and sat down to eat his supper and then toasted himself warm, and presently he went off very comfortably to sleep.

Now the King had taken a liking to Fritz and, all night, he had felt quite worried about him, so next morning he decided to come down himself from his palace to see what had happened. So, as soon as it was light, in came the King and his attendants. There lay Fritz on the ground, so still that the King was sure he must be dead.

"Alas!" said the King sorrowfully. "What a pity! A nice young fellow like that! Dead! In the flower of his youth!"

But just then Fritz sprang to his feet and, when he saw who was there, he bowed politely. The King was astonished and very much pleased.

"What sort of night did you have?" he asked.

"Oh, it went very well indeed!" said the lad and told the King about the monstrous cats and frightful dogs. "But," added he sadly, "I still don't know anything about shivering and shaking! If only someone would show me how!"

The King was delighted but he shook his head when he heard that Fritz meant to try again. However, he went back to his palace, while Fritz went back to the inn. There he spent the day as merrily as before, helping the innkeeper and his wife.

When evening came, Fritz went alone to the castle just as before, and, once again, he made a good fire and sat down on his bench. Everything was quiet until nearly midnight and then, up above, began a terrible noise of thumping and banging. Then suddenly, half a man came tumbling down the chimney into the hearth at his feet!

"Hello!" said the lad, "hello and welcome, but surely there ought to be some more of you?"

Then the noise began again and down fell the other half.

"Poor fellow," said the lad, "you seem to have had a rough journey! Sit down and warm yourself." And with that Fritz got up to make a better fire. When he looked round the two pieces had joined themselves together, and a huge and horribly ugly man was sitting on the bench where the lad had been.

"No, no," said Fritz, "that bench is mine! That stool is for you."

With that the horrible man began to yell and scream with rage and tried to push Fritz away. But the lad wouldn't allow that, and the end of it was that he forced the horrible man to fetch the stool and sit on it. Then Fritz offered him some of his food and drink, and when they had both had some supper the lad said:

"We ought to play something to pass the time till morning."

The horrible man did not answer, but, with a sudden yell, he put both his arms up the chimney and brought down a lot of bones and skulls.

"Oh," said the lad, "I see! You want to play at ninepins, and to use these skulls as balls."

And so they played, and the lad was very strict with the

201

horrible man and wouldn't let him cheat, and took no notice of how he screamed and made faces and how he even tried to strangle Fritz every time he lost. As soon as the first cocks crew and the light of morning came, the horrible man dropped into two pieces once more, and both halves, with all the skulls and bones, vanished up the chimney.

Once more the King came down in the morning from his palace to see how the lad had got on.

"I have had a jolly night of it, playing at ninepins," said Fritz and he went on to tell the King all that had happened.

"And didn't it make you shiver and shake with fear to play at ninepins with such a horrible creature as that?" asked the King.

"Oh dear no," said the lad. "We were very merry, so, alas, I still don't know how to shiver and shake."

Once more Fritz spent the day helping the good innkeeper and his wife, and once more, when it began to grow dark, he went back alone to the enchanted castle.

Now, as you know, Fritz had hardly slept at all that night because he had been playing ninepins nearly all night with the horrible man. So this time, he felt very sleepy. When he had lit his fire he looked round the room and saw something that he had not noticed before. There was a big bed in one corner.

"That bed is just what I want!" thought he, and so in he got and pulled up the bedclothes. He was just settling down comfortably, and his eyes were just shutting with sleep, when, with a terrific gust of wind, the door of the room opened of itself and the bed began moving of its own accord.

Out of the room rolled the bed and Fritz on it, and off

Fritz enjoyed this way of seeing the castle

it went with him down a dark passage. Bats flew out at
him, cold hands grabbed at him, glowing eyes stared at
him. As the bed carried him along he could see heaps of
treasure that sparkled in the moonlight and each heap
was guarded by some monster that was worse than the
last.

203

"This is a grand way to see the castle! Go faster! Go faster!" cried Fritz. At that the bed rolled on at a great pace, indeed it rolled as if six horses were harnessed to it. Up and down it bumped all over the castle, while the wind howled, the moonlight gleamed on heaps of treasure and on naked swords that slashed at him and on bats that flew out at him. Over thresholds and steps rolled the bed, and even up winding staircases, until, at last, it brought him right out into the moonlight on to the highest turret of the castle battlements. Just as the bed seemed to be going to roll right off the turret with him and plop, down into the castle moat, the first light of morning began to colour the sky and the first cocks crew. Then, with that, the bed stayed still.

"Splendid!" called out the lad. "Well done, bed! But really I still feel too sleepy to move. There are plenty of quilts and blankets here, I shall be comfortable enough," so, without even getting out to have a look, Fritz tucked himself up, turned over and went to sleep, just where he was.

Well next morning, when the King came to the great room of the castle as before, he found that this time the fire was out, and that there was no sign of the lad. The King began to feel very sorrowful, for he had hoped that, on this last morning, he would surely find him once more. He now had not much hope, but all the same he sadly ordered the soldiers who were with him, to search the castle.

"You may at least find the poor young fellow's dead body," said he.

So off the soldiers went. They went along passages, up winding stairs and down into dungeons—up they went and down they went and could find nothing.

At last one of them came up right out of the castle on to the roof and to the top of the highest turret of all. You can guess how astonished he was to see a bed up there, and the lad in it well tucked up and fast asleep. The soldier rushed down at once and told the King the good news. The King wouldn't believe it at first, so he came up to see for himself, and was delighted when he found that it was all true, and that there lay the lad fast asleep, just as the soldier and said.

"Wake up, wake up!" cried the King. "You have broken the enchantment! You are safe and sound, and now you can marry my daughter."

"Yes, Sire," said the lad, sitting up, rubbing his eyes, yawning, and looking round him in surprise, and it wasn't for a moment or two that he remembered to get up and bow to the King. "Marry the Princess! That I will gladly do," he went on, "for they tell me she is the most beautiful Princess that the sun ever shone on, and what's more, I shan't come to her as a poor man, for now I know where all these heaps of treasure are hidden. But oh dear! I still don't know what it is to shiver and shake!"

But the King only laughed, took him to the Palace, and, as they went, Fritz told him all his night's adventures. The Princess was waiting for them and she really was more beautiful than any maiden that Fritz had ever seen, and what was more, she smiled kindly at him. He was given grand clothes to wear and, next day, there was a very splendid wedding, and soon Fritz and his Princess loved each other very much.

But as time went on the Princess noticed that sometimes Fritz looked sad, so, one day, she asked him what was the matter. He told her how he had always wanted to learn how to shiver and shake, and that all his adventures in the enchanted castle hadn't helped him to learn how to do it. The Princess answered nothing to that, but, instead, she thought what she could do to help her husband to get his wish.

It was winter, and the stream that ran through the Palace garden was icy cold. One day, when her young husband sat sadly by the fire, the Princess and her maidens went out secretly. They fetched a bucketful of ice-cold water from the stream and into the bucket they put as many little, cold, wriggling fish as they could catch. Then coming in again, the Princess stole softly behind her husband and, without a word, she emptied the ice-cold water, fish and all, all down his neck and all over him.

"Don't!" he cried, jumping up. "Dear wife, what are you doing! That makes me shiver and shake!"

With that the Princess began to laugh, and all her maidens laughed too, and last of all Fritz laughed, and then he kissed the Princess tenderly.

"Thank you, thank you, dear wife!" said he. "Now, thanks to you, at last I know how to shiver and shake!"

And they lived happy ever after.

THE TOM-TIT AND THE BEAR

———— ❈ ————

ONE SUMMER DAY, THE WOLF AND THE BEAR
took a walk together in the wood.

"What can that bird be that flies about singing and
chirruping so sweetly?" asked the Bear.

"Oh," said the Wolf, "that is His Majesty the King of
the Birds."

(What was really chirruping and singing was a little
blue-tit, a Tom-tit as people often call them.)

"How I should like to see the royal palace!" exclaimed
the Bear.

"I'm afraid," said the Wolf, "that we can't see it just
yet. It isn't visiting hours. We must wait till the Queen
comes home."

Soon afterwards the Queen flew back, with food in her
beak for the fledgelings, and then she and the King
began to feed their young ones.

"Now for it!" said the Bear, who was impatient to go
and see the royal home. You see, he imagined that it
would be a gorgeous palace and that, for the first time in
his life, he would see a lot of Princes and Princesses.

"Stop a bit," said the Wolf, "we'd better wait now till
Their Majesties have gone again."

So they marked the place where they had seen the

Tom-tits fly in and out, and then they walked on a little, just to pass the time. But the Bear wanted so much to see the royal palace that he soon came back again, and, peeping among the bushes, he saw a little nest, and five young half-fledged birds lying at the bottom of it.

"But *this* isn't a royal palace!" said the Bear, who was bitterly disappointed. "I never saw such a wretched little tiny place in my life! And those aren't Royal children— not these miserable little brats!"

Now the Tom-tits heard what the Bear was saying and they were very angry, so all screamed out together:

"We're not miserable brats! This isn't a wretched little tiny place, you stupid Bear! We'll tell our Father and Mother what you said! They'll soon teach you not to be so rude!"

The five little birds all screamed so loud and snapped their beaks so angrily that the silly Bear got quite frightened, and ran away to tell the Wolf. The Wolf listened and then said that it was very serious, and that they had better run off to their caves.

The young Tom-tits kept crying and screaming; and when their father and mother came home and offered them food they all said:

"We won't touch a single worm! No, not the leg of a beetle, not even if we have to die of hunger. Not a bite will we eat, till that rude rascal of a great clumsy, shaggy Bear has been punished! He called us miserable brats and said our nest was a wretched tiny little place."

"Don't worry, my darlings," said the Tom-tit King. "I never allow anyone to be rude to my children!"

So the Tom-tit flew off and perched on a small bush right in front of the Bear's cave, and cried out in a loud but squeaky voice:

"Bruin the Bear! You have shamefully insulted our five Royal children! Because of that we hereby declare bloody and cruel war against you and yours."

The Bear never said a word, but when the Tom-tit had gone away he thought that it might be quite serious. So he called together the Ox, the Ass, the Stag, and a lot of other beasts. Meantime the Tom-tit called up, on his side, all the creatures that fly in the air, birds both great and small of course, and also a very large army of Hornets, Gnats, Wasps, Bees, Flies, and other insects.

Now that these two terrible armies had been called together, it would soon be time for the war to begin, but the Tom-tit wanted to find out who was going to be the commander-in-chief of the enemy's forces; so he quickly sent out a spy. His spy was the Gnat, who was by far the cleverest of them all, and she flew backwards and forwards to where the enemy's headquarters were, bringing back the news. She was so small that she was able to hide herself under a leaf, and indeed to get under a leaf on the very tree under which the orders of the day were being given out to the army of beasts. The Bear, who had called the army together, was standing so near the tree that the Gnat could hear every word he said. First she heard how he called to the Fox.

"Reynard," said the Bear, "you are the cleverest of all the beasts; you shall be our general and it is you who shall lead us to battle; but first we had better agree upon a few signals, so that we shall always know what you want us to do."

"Notice—" answered the Fox, in a grand tone, speaking to the whole crowd of animals and very much pleased at being made commander-in-chief, "—notice, everyone, that I have a fine long bushy tail—my Brush, as we foxes call it. It is very much like a general's plume of red feathers, don't you think? It gives me a very warlike look, as I am sure you will agree. Now remember, when you see me raise my brush in the air like this, you may be sure that I consider that the battle is going well. So, when you see that, you must all rush in to fight. On the other hand, if I drop my tail, it means that I consider that the battle is going badly and, if I keep it down, that you had all better run away as fast as you can."

As soon as the Gnat had heard all this, she flew back to the Tom-tit and told him everything.

"Aha!" said King Tom-tit. "Now I know what to do!"

The day of battle came; and, as soon as it was light, this huge army of beasts came rushing forward with such a fearful sound that the earth shook. But on the other side, His Majesty the Tom-tit, with his troops, all came flying fearlessly along against them, flapping, fluttering and beating the air, so that it was quite frightful to hear! Then both armies arranged themselves in order of battle.

Now the Tom-tit had already given special orders to his troop of Hornets. He told them that, as soon as the battle began, they were to take no notice of any other beast, but were to rush straight towards the Fox and were to fly round his tail with a terrible buzzing, and then they were all to sting his hindquarters with might and main.

The Hornets did as they were told. When Reynard felt the first sting, he jumped with the pain, but he was so brave that he only shook one of his back legs, and still kept his tail up. At the second sting he could hardly bear it and was forced to drop his brush for a moment. But when the third Hornet had stung him, he could stand it no longer, but clapped his beautiful bushy tail between his legs and scampered away as fast as he could.

As soon as the beasts saw their commander-in-chief scampering off with his tail between his legs, they thought of course, that the war must be lost, so the whole army of beasts rushed off to their homes at once, as fast as they could gallop.

So now the birds and insects found to their delight that they had won the battle!

King Tom-tit and his Queen flew back in triumph to their children and said:

"Now, children, eat, drink and be merry, for we have won a great victory!"

But the young birds said:

"No! We won't touch a thing, not a caterpillar, not a maggot! Not till the Bear himself has been here to beg our pardon."

So the King, their father, flew off to the Bear's cave.

"Villain of a Bear!" he called out, in his squeaky little voice. "Come at once to my palace, and beg my Royal children to forgive you for your insulting words! If you won't come and if you don't apologize properly, every bone in your wretched body shall be broken to pieces!"

So the Bear had to crawl out of his cave, feeling very silly, and to do what King Tom-tit had ordered him to do.

After that the young birds had a huge meal. In fact they ate everything that their parents could find to bring to them, and, if you had been there, you would have heard the whole nestful of them twittering and singing till well past midnight.

WHOEVER DOESN'T BELIEVE THIS TALE
MUST PAY A SHILLING

FOUR MUSICIANS FOR BREMEN

THERE WAS ONCE A MAN WHO HAD A DONKEY. Near a fine town called Bremen they lived. This was a good patient donkey and he carried his master's corn-sacks to the mill for many a long year. But at last there came a time when the poor beast's strength began to go, and he couldn't carry the heavy sacks without stumbling. He was a wise old beast who could see that his master was beginning to wonder how he might best save on donkey-keep. He decided not to wait, so one night, with one jerk of his head, he broke his halter, and set out on the road to Bremen.

"I'm far the best musician on the farm," said he to himself, "and in Bremen they have a town-band. They'll be glad to have me!" So on he walked, and soon he found a big dog lying panting on the road, as if it had run far and fast.

"Why are you panting, big fellow?" asked the donkey.

The dog answered: "I am getting old. Running doesn't agree with me—I'm no good for hunting any more. I got the idea that my master meant to get rid of me, so I ran off—but what now? How am I to earn my keep?"

"I'll tell you what," said the donkey. "I'm going to Bremen. They've got a splendid town-band there and I shall be one of the musicians. Why don't you come with me? You could be a musician too!"

The dog agreed to this excellent plan, so on they went together. Before long they came to a cat, sitting on the path, with a face like three rainy days.

"Now then, old girl, what's gone askew with you?" asked the donkey.

"I'm getting old," answered the cat, "and instead of hunting for mice, all I want to do is to sit by the fire. I heard my mistress say that she was going to drown me, so I ran away. That was all very well, but now where am I to go?"

"Come with us to Bremen. They've got a splendid town-band, and as you understand night-music they're sure to be glad to have you. You can be a town-musician."

The cat thought it over for a bit, decided that it was a good idea, and went with them. So now there were three musicians on the road for Bremen.

Then they came to a farm-yard where the cock was sitting perched on the gate, crowing with all his might.

The donkey laid back his long ears in pain.

"Good gracious, what a noise! Your crow quite goes through my head," said he. "What's the matter?"

"I'm really foretelling fine weather, because it is the day on which Our Lady washes the Christ-child's little shirts, and she wants to dry them," said the cock. "But that's not the only reason. Some visitors are coming for Sunday, and I heard my mistress tell the cook that she wants me made into soup, so I thought I'd better crow at the top of my voice while I still can."

"Poor old red-comb!" said the donkey. "You'd far better come away with us. We're going to Bremen to join the town band. You've got a capital voice."

The cock agreed to this plan, so now there were four of

them, donkey, dog, cat and cock, all on the road to Bremen.

Now Bremen was still quite a long way off, and they knew they couldn't possibly get there in one day. By evening they had got as far as a forest, so the donkey and the dog lay down under a large tree while the cat and the cock climbed and flew and finally settled themselves in the branches.

It was the cock who went the highest and, when he was right up, he looked round and, far away in the distance, he thought he saw a little spark of light; so he called down:

"There must be a house not far off. I can see a light."

"We had better go and have a look," said the wise donkey.

The dog and the cat thought so too, for they were hungry. The donkey had had a grass-supper and the cock had found something or other to peck, but the cat and dog thought that a few bones, if possible with some meat on them, would do them good.

Then they all made their way as quietly as they could towards the place where the light was. At last they found that they had come to quite a big well-lighted house. But who, except some poor woodman or a charcoal-burner, would live in such an out of the way place? The donkey, who was the biggest, went to the window and looked in.

"What do you see, my grey horse?" whispered the cock.

"I see a table covered with good things to eat," answered the donkey in the same low tone, "and my guess is that it's a gang of robbers sitting round enjoying themselves."

"If only we were in there instead of out here!" said the cat, licking her whiskers.

Then the animals went back into the forest for a counsel of war. They would have to drive away the robbers; but how? At last they thought of a plan. The donkey, as the biggest, was to stand with his front hooves on the window-ledge, the dog, who was the next biggest, was to jump on to the donkey's back, the cat was to climb up on to the dog, and, lastly, the cock was to fly up and perch on the cat's head.

So this is what they did, and then, when the donkey gave the signal, they began their splendid musical performance: the donkey brayed, the dog barked, the cat caterwauled, and the cock crowed so hard he nearly split. Then, when the noise was at its most deafening, they all leaned forward and toppled bang through the window into the room, shattering the glass.

At the horrible din, the robbers had already sprung up, and when this mountain of yelling creatures tumbled into the room, right on the top of them, they all fled, in a great fright, out into the forest.

The animals saw that the coast was now clear, and the four of them, well pleased, sat down at the table and ate and drank to their hearts' content.

As soon as they had finished up the eatables the four musicians decided that they would put out the light, but before doing so, each found a sleeping-place according to his nature. The donkey went outside and lay down on a nice heap of straw in the yard, the dog decided on a mat he had found behind the door, the cat curled up on the hearth where she got heat from the warm ashes, and the cock flew up and perched himself upon a roof beam.

So, one by one, they all fell asleep. When it was past midnight, the robbers—who hadn't gone far—could see that there was no longer a light in their house.

"We ought not to have let ourselves be frightened out of our wits! One of you had better go and see what really happened in the house!" said the captain.

So the boldest robber went off as silently as he could. Finding that everything was still, he went into the kitchen. There was still a little light from the remains of the fire, and he stooped down, meaning—so as to get a little more light—to blow at what he took to be two bright sparks. But what he thought were bright sparks were really the glistening, fiery eyes of the cat, and, when he blew in her face in that rude way, the cat was very angry indeed, and flew at him, spitting and scratching. The robber, who couldn't think what had attacked him, was dreadfully frightened, ran to the back-door and, in his fright, trod on the dog who lay there. The dog instantly jumped up and bit his leg. The robber ran on across the yard and when he came to the heap of straw the donkey gave him a kick on his other shin.

"Cock-a-doodle-doo!" cried the cock from the beam, awakened by the noise. "Cock a doodle doo!"

The terrified robber ran back to his captain.

"Captain," he cried, "the house is in a terrible state! There's a horrible witch in the kitchen who spat at me and scratched my face with her long claws. By the door stands a man with a knife, who stabbed me in the leg; in the yard there lies a dreadful monster who beat me with a wooden club; and up on the roof, sits the judge, who kept calling out, 'Bring him up to me-ee! Bring him up to me-ee!' Indeed, Captain, I was lucky to get away with my life!"

After hearing this shocking tale the robbers never dared to use their house again, but moved off to a new district.

As for the four victorious musicians who had meant to go to Bremen, when they searched the house by daylight they found both provisions and money in the cupboards. Altogether the house suited them so well that they could not decide to leave it. As they are probably living there to this day, we shall never know whether the Bremen town-band would have been glad of their help. Or not?

THE GOOSE-GIRL AT THE WELL

One fine morning long ago, a handsome and good-natured young Count was striding along through a meadow. The birds sang, the leaves rustled, the first cool breezes of autumn made travelling easy, so that the young man felt happy and he whistled and sang as he went. Not far from the path, he saw an old woman who was cutting grass with a sickle. She had a sack near her into which she was putting the cut grass and, near the sack, stood two big baskets, one full of rosy apples and one full of yellow and russet pears.

"Good morning, Granny," said the young Count.

"And a good morning to you," answered she.

"You're surely not going to try to carry that great sack and those two heavy baskets all by yourself?" says he.

"I've got to carry them, dear Sir," says she. "Rich folk's children, like you, can't carry loads, I know, but we poor folk have to."

"Well, I hope you haven't got far to take it," says he.

"Why not come with me and see?" says she. "You'd soon get there with your straight back and your young legs, even if you are a rich man's son! It's true that this morning I have got rather a big load for a poor old woman so perhaps you could take the sack, while I take the two baskets? It's only a little way! Not far off your path."

The young man laughed. "All right, it's a lovely morning," says he, "and if it's only to show you that a Count's son can carry a load just as well as a peasant's son, I'll come along and give you a hand."

Almost before he had finished speaking, the old woman had hoisted the sack of grass on to the young man's back and, what is more, she had tied it on pretty firmly.

"I don't suppose you're strong enough to carry the apples and pears as well?" said she.

The young man didn't like being thought weak, so he said yes to that too. But when she began to tell him that it wouldn't take the like of a nice young fellow like him more than an hour or so to get to her house, and when she pointed the way, straight up the steep mountain-side, he began to think the joke was going rather too far. However he didn't like to say anything, so off they walked.

"You see," said she, chattering away as before, "the load isn't heavy at all!"

"You're wrong there! It's very heavy indeed," answered the young Count rather crossly. "I don't believe this sack is really full of grass at all! It must be full of cobble-stones, it's such a weight! As for your apples and pears, I believe they must be made of lead."

"Ah, that's just your fun!" said the old dame, laughing.

"So it's a couple of hours now, is it?" thought the young man. However, he still didn't say anything.

After struggling along for a while, up and up, on a path so rough and steep that half the loose stones on it seemed to roll away under his feet, the young man felt so puffed and out of breath and his heart was pounding so much that he stopped.

"A joke's a joke," said he, "but this one isn't a joke at

218

all! Help me off with the sack! I won't carry it a step farther."

But the old woman only laughed the more.

"You were ready enough with fine words, my lad," said she. "Now you can step out. I shan't help you off with the load!" And when the young man tried to get it off himself, he found that she had tied it on so firmly that, somehow, he couldn't shift it at all. It really seemed to be stuck on his back for good, and the more he tried to get rid of it the more the old woman laughed.

"Don't be so cross, dear sir! Carry your load patiently, and when you get it to my cottage, I'll give you a good reward. Save your breath for walking! Why, you're getting as red in the face as a turkey-cock!"

Well, he still didn't like being laughed at and anyhow he couldn't, try as he would, get the sack off his back, so on he trudged, in no very good temper. Up and up the mountain they went with the sack seeming to get heavier and heavier and the old woman jumping about behind him urging him along, sometimes with her teasing words and sometimes with a good sharp prod.

Suddenly, what did the mocking old dame do, but actually spring up on to the top of the sack herself! There she sat and, though she had looked as if she might be as light as a withered apple, now he found that she was really as heavy as if she had been a strong man. The poor young Count's knees began to tremble, his heart was pounding harder than ever and the perspiration was pouring off him when, at long last, they really did come in sight of her cottage.

It was a pretty little house, and it lay in the middle of a small meadow in the lap of the mountains. A large flock of white geese had just been driven into this meadow from

219

the other side of the cottage, and, as soon as they saw the old woman, all the geese came flapping and cackling to greet her, all with their long necks stretched out.

Behind the flock of geese there walked a very strange creature, tall and strong like any well-grown country girl, but with the grey wrinkled face of an ugly old woman, and with not even a scrap of hair to be seen under her kerchief.

"Good evening, dear child," the little old dame called out to this queer-looking goose-girl, and with that she jumped nimbly off the top of the sack of grass. "This kind gentleman has been carrying all my load for me and he was so good that he even took me on his back as well! Wasn't he kind! We've had a fine time! Cracking jokes all the way!" As she was speaking she was at last taking the great sack off the young man's back. And now, looking at him kindly, instead of mockingly, she said:

"You've fairly earned your wages, young man! Sit down on the bench and rest yourself." Then turning to the goose-girl she went on: "Go into the house now, dear child, I can't leave you alone with a nice young gentleman! He might fall in love with you!"

The Count was amused by this.

"What a dreadful sort of sweetheart!" he thought to himself, taking another look at her leathery face. He noticed that, while the goose-girl went obediently into the house, the old woman began to stroke and fondle each goose as if it, like the goose-girl, had been one of her children.

Soon the young Count began to feel better and, as he looked about him, he couldn't help thinking that, in spite of everything, it certainly was delightful up here. The leaves on the fruit-trees that stood near the cottage had hardly begun to turn, the air was warm and mild and a thousand flowers grew among the grasses of the meadow. Through the green and flowery grass ran a little sparkling brook in which the white geese were paddling with their broad yellow feet. Presently the old dame came back, and he saw that she was holding something in her hand.

"I certainly treated you hardly," said she, smiling. "But you know, it hasn't killed you after all! I've been in doubt what your reward should be, for you are one that has no need of money or land, so at last I decided on this." With that she put a great emerald into his hand, and when he looked closely at it he saw that it was in the form of a little box-shaped book, and that, hinges and all, it was cut out of a single precious stone that shone greener than the grass.

"It will bring you good fortune," said she.

Thanking the queer old woman for her present, the Count stood up, said good-bye and set off again, for, strangely enough, he now felt as fresh as when he had set out early that morning. So off he strode down the mountain and he never so much as looked back to see if he could again catch sight of the strange, ugly goose-girl.

It was not till a day or two later that he reached a large town, for, though the path up the mountain had been steep and rough, it had been easy enough to find with the old woman prodding and guiding him, but now, going down, he had somehow missed it.

When he got to this fine town he went at once to pay his respects to the old King and Queen who ruled over that part of the country, and, as he had no other present, he knelt before her and laid the little emerald box at the Queen's feet.

She told him to rise and to put the beautiful thing into

221

He knelt before the Queen

her hand, so that she could see it better. No sooner had she had a good look at it than she saw how to open the tiny box, and, looking inside, she fell back in a dead faint.

— 2 —

Late that night the old Queen sent secretly for the young Count and when they were alone she told him a strange story.

She told him that she and the King had once had three beautiful daughters, and that the youngest had been so lovely that all the world looked at her in wonder, and that whenever she cried, pearls, instead of tears, fell from her eyes, but that three years ago, the King, feeling himself to be growing old, thought he had better decide how his Kingdom was to be divided, and what marriage portions each of the princesses was to have. He had called his three daughters, and said he knew that they all loved him, but that he would like whichever loved him the best to have the largest portion. One had answered that she loved him as much as the sweetest sugar, the next that she loved him more than she loved her prettiest dresses, but the youngest had only said in a low voice that of course she loved her father. At that quiet answer the old King had fallen into a passion, had divided the Kingdom between the two eldest and, in spite of the poor Queen's tears and prayers, he had chased the youngest one away.

The King soon repented of this foolish and wicked deed, but in vain had he sent out his guards to find the lost Princess. The whole Kingdom, forests, mountains, and all, had been searched to no purpose, and though the Queen had long tried to hope that the Princess might still be alive, she too had at last given her up for dead.

"And now, today," went on the Queen, "when I opened your emerald box I saw that, in it, was a pearl exactly like one of those that used to fall from her eyes when she cried. Tell me at once how you got this strange box."

So the young Count told the Queen the whole tale, first and last, but added that, except the old dame and the strange and ugly goose-girl, he had seen no living soul during the time he had been at the cottage in the lap of the mountain.

It was not long before the Queen sent him to bed, and then she went and told the King the young Count's story. So it was resolved that they should all three set out next day to try to find the old woman's cottage in the hope that she might be able to give them some news of the lost Princess. The King and Queen could not help hoping that, where the pearl had been, they might at least get some news.

On the very day and at the very time when the young Count had laid the precious emerald box before the Queen, up in the cottage, the old dame and the ugly goose-girl had been sitting spinning. Suddenly, though it was not yet dark, an owl fluttered against the window, and stared in at them for all the world as if it brought a message to the two women, and the strange goose-girl nodded.

Next evening, after she had brought back the geese from their pasture, the ugly goose-girl went out alone. It was a bright moonlight night. Across the meadow she went, and down towards the valley, till she came to a certain ancient well with an old oak tree leaning over it. First she took off her kerchief and shook down a mass of long golden hair, and after that she did a very strange thing. She took off a closely fitting leather mask which had entirely hidden her face. How she was changed!

Anyone who had been there to see her, in the moonlight, would have seen that now her eyes were as bright as stars, her cheeks were as pink and fine as apple-blossom and her lips were like twin cherries. She hung the ugly mask on a bush and stooped to wash her face at the well, but no sooner had she begun than she looked up startled, for she thought she heard a creaking in the oak tree. So frightened was she, that, without thinking what she was doing, she sprang up the path that led to the cottage, running all the way and jumping from stone to stone as swift and graceful as a roe-deer. She felt nervous because she was without her disguise, and in her hurry, she left her leather mask behind.

The goose-girl without her mask

When she opened the cottage door, the old dame was waiting for her. The poor girl trembled to think that she had got to own up to having left the leather mask behind.

But the old woman only smiled, stopped her when she tried to explain, and said that she knew all about it already.

By now it was nearly midnight, not at all the time when the house was usually cleaned, and yet, to her surprise, the girl noticed, by the light of a bright log fire that, while she had been out at the well, the old woman had been busy sweeping, scrubbing and polishing.

"Mother, why do you clean the house at this time of the night?"

"All must be clean and sweet for what is to come," was the answer.

The girl felt uneasy. "What is to come?" she asked.

"It's three years to the very day since you came to me. We can stay together no longer!" said the old woman.

"Don't cast me off, dear mother!" cried the poor girl. "I have no friends and no home to go to! I have worked my best for you and always been obedient. Don't send me out into the wide world again!"

"Nay, little daughterkin, I'll not do that!" said the old woman lovingly, and she laid her old gnarled hand on the girl's golden head. "Never fear! You'll soon find better company than an old woman and a gaggle of geese."

"But I don't want to leave you! I love you and the geese too!" said the girl.

But the old dame only shook her head and went on with her work again.

"At least tell me what's to happen?" begged the girl.

"Enough questions!" said the old woman. "The house must be clean! Leave me to get on with my work. Go to your room, comb your hair, take off your goose-girl dress and put on the silk gown in which you first came to me."

— 3 —

Now perhaps you may be wondering what it was that had made the oak tree down by the well creak so loudly that it made the girl so frightened as to run away and leave her leather mask behind? The oak tree had given a creak because of a sudden movement made by the young Count. He had been searching about, had seen someone coming along in the moonlight, and had hidden himself in the branches of the oak. He had been so startled when he

226

saw the change that had come over the ugly goose-girl that he had moved a little in his hiding-place. He had not been able to see very well, but he felt sure that he had caught a glimpse of golden hair, a sweet face, and a pair of sparkling blue eyes. Perhaps the search might be near its end? But before he had time to speak to her, the girl had fled away. However, he knew which path the old King and Queen had meant to take, so, as soon as the lovely girl had disappeared, the young man rushed off to find them to tell them what he had seen and to lead them to the cottage in the lap of the mountains.

So, he and the King and Queen all made their way as quickly as they could to the cottage from which a light still shone. They did not knock at the door, but all three stood outside looking in at the window. There, sure enough, sat the old dame, quietly spinning, nodding her head, but never looking round.

The room was so clean and everything was so bright that it looked as if the little mist men, who carry no dust on their feet, must live here. But there seemed to be only the old woman and not a trace of either an ugly goose-girl or of a lovely lost princess.

As they watched they saw the old woman get up and, in a moment, though they still had not knocked, she had opened the door to them.

"Come in and rest," said she. "I know you all, already!"

Now the old King and Queen were so tired with the climb up to the cottage that they were glad to sit down on the bench by the brightly burning wood fire.

"You might have spared yourselves much sorrow and a long walk," said the old woman, looking severely at the King, "if you had not unjustly driven away the daughter who loved you best! However, you have been lucky. No harm has come to her. For three years she has been here in the mountains with me, looking after my geese, and here she has learned no evil. As for you, you have been punished enough already by the sight of your sad Queen and by your own remorse!" With that the old dame went to the door of the inner room and called:

"Come out, little daughter!"

When the Princess stepped out in her silken dress and with her golden hair round her shoulders she looked so lovely that it was as if the sun had broken through the clouds. She went up to her father and mother and embraced them tenderly. As for the young Count he was struck dumb by the sight of her beauty and gazed at her so fixedly that, when she saw it, she blushed as pink as a moss-rose.

At last, when they had talked for a while, the King said sadly to his daughter:

"Dearest of my children! What shall I do? I have divided my Kingdom between your two sisters and now I have nothing left to give you."

"She needs nothing," said the old woman. "I saved the pearls that the poor thing wept because of all your unkindness, and they are so many that now they make up more than the worth of your whole Kingdom. Besides the pearls, as payment for her services to me, I mean to give her this little house."

No sooner had she said this than the old woman vanished. At once it seemed to them that the walls rattled a little, and then, when everything was still again, it seemed to them that they were standing in the hall of a splendid castle.

.   .   .   .

Now this story used to be told, long ago, by a very old lady, and when she had got as far as that, she always told us that she had forgotten the rest. But I have always believed that the Princess married the young Count, that they went on living up there among the apple trees and by the sparkling stream in the lap of the mountain, and that they were very happy.

I used to wonder if the geese (who, so she used to tell us, disappeared at the same time as the old woman and whom the old woman seemed to have loved as if they had been her children) really were other girls or Princesses who had been enchanted and whom she had also befriended. Be all that as it may, we always believed that the old woman was either a white-witch or perhaps the lost Princess's fairy godmother.

THE VALIANT LITTLE TAILOR

ONE SUMMER EVENING, IN A FAR AWAY TIME, A
little tailor was cheerfully stitching away at a suit of clothes
by his open window. He sat cross-legged on his big table,
as tailors always did in those days. Just in reach, but out
of the way of his nice clean work, he had laid something
very good, and as he stitched, he kept looking at it out of
the corner of his eye.

It was a big slice of bread, cut right across a very large
loaf. On it he had spread a thick layer of some particularly
nice jam, and he was looking forward to eating it. This
delicious treat lay all ready on a plate and as he stitched
away he could smell the jam distinctly. He meant to eat
the whole big slice as soon as ever he came to the end of
the seam on which he was working, for that seam was
the last one on a whole suit of clothes.

But he had forgotten that there were others, both in the
room and outside his window, who also thought that the
jam smelt good. Soon, as he stitched, he saw out of the
corner of his eye, that a regular cloud of flies had begun
to buzz round his lovely bread-and-jam and that the
boldest flies were beginning to settle on it, and to eat the
jam. The tailor wasn't going to put up with that sort of
impudence!

"Get off!" cried he, but still sewing away. "Who invited you!" But the flies didn't understand a word of German, which was the language that the little tailor spoke, so, though he said it again—and more too and even louder—the flies took not the slightest notice of his order, but only buzzed the more. Dozens of flies had begun to settle on the jam to which he had been so much looking forward.

"Get off, you brutes!" cried the little tailor in a really furious tone. With that, he at last stopped his busy sewing, reached down to a box under the table where he kept his oddments, pulled out a stout bit of cloth and crying: "I'll give it you!" he gave a tremendous swipe at the flies. Most of them managed to buzz off, but afterwards, when he looked on the table, the tailor was delighted to see that several flies lay on their backs, dead. Feeling very much as if he were a general, the tailor began to count his fallen enemies.

"One, two, three, four, five, six, seven! What a fine fellow I am to be sure!" said the tailor to himself. "Why, I killed seven at a single blow! Who dares to say that tailors are no good at fighting? I must let the whole world know what a splendid victory I've won!" So what did the little tailor do? As soon as he had folded up the suit he had just finished, eaten the bread and jam and licked his fingers clean, he pulled out bits from his oddment box till he found what he wanted, and then he set to work to make himself a belt. When it was done he embroidered these four words on it in large letters:

SEVEN AT A BLOW!

He felt so full of delicious bread and jam, so pleased with himself, so delighted with his beautiful new belt, that he resolved that he would be a tailor no longer, but would

231

put on his belt, shut up his shop and go out into the Wide World to seek his fortune and the sooner the better!

As he took a last look round his house he caught sight, on the back of a shelf in a cupboard, of a small soft round cottage cheese. Thinking that this cheese might come in useful in the Wide World, he popped it into his pocket. Then he went out of his door, and he locked it carefully behind him. As he did so he noticed a sort of fluttering in a gooseberry bush and saw that a bird had got tangled up in an old bit of netting. Thinking that this bird might also be useful in the Wide World, he caught it, and into his pocket it went, along with the old round cheese.

Now though he was a nimble little fellow, till this very day the tailor had led such a quiet busy life, that he had never once set foot outside the town. So now, once he got out into the country, he was surprised at all that he saw. Trees, grass, flowers, everything seemed new and delightful! In front of him he saw a mountain and, thinking that he would really be able to see the Wide World from the top, he took a path that seemed to lead towards it. On he walked, up and up, and as he walked he whistled and sang because everything was so new and pleasant. Though the path was really very steep, he was such a light, spry little man, that he didn't feel in the least tired.

What was his surprise, however, when, right at the top of the mountain, he saw an enormous giant who was sitting there very comfortably, admiring the view. But though the tailor was surprised at seeing such an enormous creature (for this really was a particularly big and powerful giant), he wasn't in the least frightened, but went boldly up to the great fellow.

"Good day, friend!" says the tailor to the giant. "You

look very comfortable sitting there, and looking out over the Wide World."

The giant didn't answer and scarcely looked at the tailor. It seemed as if he didn't care to speak to such a ridiculous little person. However, the tailor went on chattering away cheerfully.

"Into the Wide World! That's where I'm going—just to try my luck, you know. Why don't you come along too?"

"Come along with a miserable little mannikin like you?" answered the giant in his great rumbling voice. "What an idea!"

"Miserable little mannikin indeed!" said the tailor indignantly, drawing himself up to his full small height, sticking out his chest and unbuttoning his coat. "Just you take a look at that, old fellow, before you start calling me names!"

At last the giant peered down to see the words that were written on the belt, for the indignant little man kept pointing at them. As you know, the words were:

SEVEN AT A BLOW!

When he read that, the giant began to scratch his head; he thought, you see, that the words must mean that the little tailor had killed seven men at one blow. All the same, thought he, even if the seven had been men, such a slender tiny little fellow couldn't possibly be a match for giants, not even for one giant. So then the giant put down his great hand and picked up a stone.

"Can you do this?" asked the giant, squeezing the stone in his enormous fist till drops of water oozed out of it.

"Of course I can!" answered the valiant little tailor. "That sort of thing's only child's play to a fellow like me!"

and with that the tailor put his hand into his pocket, pulled out the old soft cheese (which really did look very much like a round stone) and squeezed it till quite a stream of whey ran out of it.

"There! That's more than you got out of your old stone!" said the tailor in triumph when he saw how surprised the giant seemed.

The giant didn't know what to say to that, but all the same he thought he would try something else. So standing up, he picked up another stone and then hurled it up into the sky. The stone went so high that it went right out of sight and it was quite a long time before it came down again, thump, at their feet.

"Can you do that?" asked the giant, well pleased with himself. He felt quite sure that he had beaten the little tailor this time.

"That? That was nothing! Your stone came down

again! But just you watch now! I'll throw one so high it won't come down at all!" Once more the tailor reached into his pocket, took hold of the bird and threw it into the air with all his might. Up and away flew the bird, delighted to be free.

"You certainly can throw!" said the puzzled giant. "Now let's see if you know how to carry things properly."

Well the little tailor agreed to have one more trial, so the two set off down the other side of the mountain till they came to a little wood. Here lay a huge oak-tree, ready felled, but with all its branches and twigs still on it.

"Just lend me a hand carrying this tree to my cave," said the giant. "I'm a bit short of fire-wood."

"With all my heart!" answered the tailor. "Just take the trunk on your shoulder and I'll take the end with the twigs and branches—that's a lot heavier!"

The giant, suspecting nothing, stooped down at once and heaved up the thick, heavy trunk on to his shoulder, just as the tailor had hoped he would. Once the thick trunk lay like that, the giant couldn't turn his head to see what was happening at the other end of the tree, so, what should the tailor do but hop up on to one of the branches.

So now, there was the stupid giant plodding off towards his cave carrying the whole tree and the little tailor into the bargain. Soon the tailor, who was thoroughly enjoying himself, began to whistle and sing, and the song he sang was called, "Three Tailors Rode Out at the Gate".

The giant who was beginning to puff and blow with the whole weight of the tree, listened to the singing in amazement. He thought the tailor really must be very strong if, while he was carrying the branched end of the tree, he had all that breath left for singing. Soon the giant began to be tired of the whole business, and so he called out over his shoulder:

"Hey you behind there! I'm going to let the tree-trunk fall."

Hearing that, the tailor jumped nimbly off his branch, and when the giant had got rid of the trunk, and could turn his head and look round again, there stood the tailor with his legs apart and his two arms round a branch, looking for all the world as if he had been helping all the time.

"Fancy a great fellow like you not being able to carry one end of a tree like this!" said the tailor, leaving go of the branch, and dusting his hands together. "Good evening to you! I can see that I shall do better trying my luck in the Wide World if I go by myself!"

So saying, the nimble little man went off through the

wood as fast as his legs would carry him, so that, when at
last the stupid giant guessed that, somehow or other, he
had been tricked, and when he began to shout and to hunt
about angrily for him, the valiant little tailor had got
away safely.

— 2 —

On went the little tailor, out into the Wide World,
always following his own pointed nose.

After he had walked for a long time he came in sight of a
great walled castle, and when he had had a good look at it
from the outside of the walls, he lay down on a patch of
grass just outside the great gate. But, as he settled himself
to sleep, he took care to open his coat, so that anyone who
happened to pass by would be able to read the words that
were embroidered on his belt:

SEVEN AT A BLOW!

He hadn't slept long before quite a crowd had collected,
and soon someone went off to call two of the King's
wisest advisers to come and have a look at the sleeping
stranger.

"I wonder what a great warrior like this is doing here in
peace time?" said the first of these wise advisers, when
he had read what was written on the belt.

"He must be a very great Lord indeed!" said the
second when he too had stooped and read the words. So
then the two wise councillors went back into the castle to
tell the King about what they had seen. The King asked
what they thought he had better do.

"Our advice to your Majesty," said they, "is that this
stranger be persuaded to stay here. If war should break
out, and we should have to defend the castle, he would,
no doubt, be a very useful man to have on our side."

The King quite agreed with this excellent advice, and immediately sent one of his courtiers to go to the sleeping stranger and to sit by him, without of course disturbing him. As soon as the great warrior woke, however, the courtier was to offer him a post in the King's garrison. So, when the little tailor began to stretch himself and to open his eyes, the courtier, bowing deeply, gave him the King's message and begged him to consent to join the garrison.

The Tailor kindly consents to join the garrison

"I came here for that very purpose!" said the little tailor grandly. "Tell His Majesty that I shall be delighted to help him!" And so it came about that the little tailor was received with great honour and was given a high post in the Royal garrison.

But the other soldiers and officers didn't like having someone who could kill seven at a blow as one of their comrades.

"What are we to do?" they muttered among themselves. "Suppose he doesn't like us? Or suppose, by ill luck, one of us should happen to disobey one of his orders? Or suppose he should just lose his temper over something and should begin to lay about him? Why, seven of us would die at each blow!"

So the soldiers and officers of the garrison went to the King in a body. Then the wisest of them stepped forward and saluted.

"Your Majesty," said he, "we all beg to be honourably discharged from your service! We are not prepared to serve any longer with a man who kills seven at a blow."

Now the King didn't like to hear this. He didn't want to lose the whole of his faithful garrison, and he began to wish that he had never set eyes on the terrible stranger. But of course, thought the King, it would be too dangerous now just to dismiss a man like that. Who could tell what such a terrible fellow might do! The King worried for a long time what was to be done, but, at last, he thought of a plan.

So next morning a courtier came to the little tailor and, bowing low, told him that he had a message from the King.

"I am always at His Majesty's command!" answered the little tailor in his new grand way.

"You must know," said the courtier, "that, in a forest not far off, there live two extremely troublesome giants who keep coming out of their caves to rob, ravage, and burn. They are terrible fellows and, so far, no one has been able to get the better of them. His Majesty now thinks, however, that to send such a great warrior as yourself out against them, would be his best chance of getting rid of them. He therefore offers you a hundred

239

mounted men to help in the work and a splendid reward. If you are successful, this reward will be the hand of his daughter in marriage and half his kingdom."

The little tailor looked thoughtful when he heard this. He didn't altogether like the idea of tackling two giants at once, but then he thought that, after all, it wasn't every day that a tailor was offered half a kingdom and the hand of a beautiful princess. So, without any more thinking he agreed, then and there, that he would try his luck.

"But," added he, "please tell the King that I shall not need the hundred men that he so kindly offers. 'SEVEN AT A BLOW' is my motto, so I expect that I shall have no difficulty if, as you say, there are only two of these giants."

So, next day, the little tailor set out, but the hundred mounted men followed him—just in case. However, when he got to the outskirts of the forest where the giants were supposed to be, he told the captain and his men to wait, as he preferred to do what had to be done by himself.

"Good-bye! I'll soon finish them off! Never fear!" he exclaimed and, so saying, he bounded off nimbly among the trees. He hadn't gone far when he heard a curious rumbling, and creeping softly up he saw that all this noise was made by the two giants who both lay, fast asleep, under a big stout tree and who were both snoring to such an extent that, stout as the tree was, its branches waved up and down.

The little tailor hid himself and watched the sleeping giants for a while, considering what he would do. Then, very quietly, he began to hunt about till he had gathered a pocketful of stones, some large and some small. When he thought he had got enough, the light little man climbed quickly up the large tree and sat himself down comfortably (and well hidden) astride a branch which stretched out just above where the two great creatures lay snoring. Then, taking careful aim, he began to let a few of his stones fall on to the chest of the first giant. For a time nothing happened, the snoring just went on as before, but at the fourth stone the first giant began to stir and grumble in his sleep, and at last he sat up and gave the second giant a hard push.

"Do be quiet!" said the first giant. "For goodness' sake stop knocking on my chest!"

"You've been dreaming, stupid!" said the second giant. "No one's been knocking on your chest, you great donkey!"

After a bit more grumbling and name-calling, they both lay down again. But before they could really settle off to sleep, the tailor let quite a fair-sized stone drop, this time on to the chest of the second giant.

"Do stop it, you ass!" said the second giant, rubbing the place.

"Stop what?" muttered the first giant, yawning.

"Stop pelting me!" said the second giant crossly.

After a bit more grumbling and a bit more name-calling the pair of them tried to settle down again. Then the little tailor began his game again, and at last, picking up the biggest stone of all, he threw it down with all his might on to the chest of the first giant.

"You brute! This is really too bad!" shouted the giant, springing up in a fury and, with that, he began to pound the second giant with a pair of fists as big as hams.

Up sprang the second giant in a rage and began to defend himself. Soon they were both so angry that they were going at it with their fists like two madmen, so that all round them the trees snapped.

"I hope this tree doesn't break!" thought the little tailor. But luckily for him it was the stoutest tree of all and so it only shook; but even then the little tailor had to hold on for his very life whenever the two great cumbersome creatures lurched against it. Soon the two giants got more furious still and began to root up trees to use as clubs. Blood began to flow, and the end of the battle was that each hit the other one so hard with these uprooted trees that they both fell senseless to the ground. As soon as he saw this the little tailor jumped down from his branch, drew out his sword, and in a moment he had finished them both off as they lay stunned and helpless.

Then, quite at his ease, he wiped his sword, put it up in its scabbard again, and strolled quietly back to where the hundred soldiers were waiting by their tethered horses.

"The work is done!" said the valiant little tailor to the captain and to the men, who had all gathered round him. "Hard work it was! Come and see how they even tore up trees while they tried to defend themselves! But of course whatever they could do was all no good. It isn't so easy, even for giants, to defend themselves from a man who kills SEVEN AT A BLOW!"

"But aren't you even wounded?" cried the captain in astonishment.

"Oh, don't worry about me," answered the little tailor grandly. "Those giants couldn't even disarrange my hair!"

So then he led the hundred soldiers into the forest. Sure enough, there lay the two giants, covered with blood and with the earth all trampled and with snapped and torn-up trees all round them.

So back to the King they all rode in triumph and then of course, to the King's vexation, the tailor asked for the promised reward.

— 3 —

"Before I give you my daughter's hand and half my kingdom," said the King, who still hoped to get rid of the terrible tailor, "I should like you to do one more heroic deed. You are such a great warrior and have managed so well with those giants (never even getting a wound) that I'm sure you'll find this new task quite easy!"

"What is it?" asked the little tailor.

"In another part of the forest," answered the crafty King, "there lurks a furious unicorn, the kind of unicorn that will even fight against a lion. This is a beast which does great harm. But, as unicorns are also rare and beautiful creatures, I should like you to bring it back alive."

"I fear one unicorn even less than I feared the two giants," said the valiant little tailor. " 'SEVEN AT A BLOW!' That's the sort of fighter I am!"

So once more the tailor set off. This time, instead of a sword, he took with him a rope and an axe and, once more, as soon as they had got to the forest, he told the soldiers who had been sent with him, to wait. Again he went on alone, his rope and his axe at the ready, looking and spying about to right and left to see if he could find the furious unicorn. He really had no need to look; for one thing the unicorn was white, and for another it wasn't at all inclined to hide. Indeed it came rushing straight at him as if it meant to drive its long sharp horn right through the poor little man.

"Gently, gently!" cried the valiant tailor, standing quite still. "It can't be done as quickly as that!" But on rushed the snorting, galloping beast. Still the valiant little tailor stood his ground, but, just as the unicorn

The unicorn rushed furiously at the tailor

had nearly reached him, he stepped nimbly behind the tree in front of which he had been standing. The unicorn was galloping at such a pace that it couldn't possibly stop itself, so that it ran full tilt against the tree, almost stunned itself, and drove its long twisted horn so hard into the tree-trunk that it couldn't draw it out again.

"Now I've got you!" cried the little tailor, coming out from behind the tree. With that he quickly put a loop of rope round its neck and then, with a blow or two with the axe, he managed to loosen the horn out of the tree-trunk. Then of course he had nothing to do but to join the soldiers again and lead the half-stunned beast in triumph to the King.

Now the King was glad enough to have the unicorn, but he was sorely vexed to have back the tailor, and he didn't in the least want to give him the promised reward. However, this time the King did go so far as to order a few wedding preparations to be begun. Then he suggested to the tailor that, while the wedding was being got ready, there was just one more heroic deed that he might care to do while they were waiting.

"This one is quite simple for a great warrior like you," said the King. "It's really only a little hunting expedition. I should like you to help to get rid of a wild boar that lives in the marshes and is rather a trouble to the farmers round about. Of course you shall have the help of my regular huntsmen, and when you have got rid of the beast, I promise you that there shall be no more delay. As you can see for yourself, I've had the wedding preparations begun already, so you needn't worry."

"Oh, if it's merely hunting a wild boar this time," said the little tailor, "that will be child's play to me!"

Now the fact was that this boar was a huge and frightful beast. It had its lair in a part of the marshes near which, on a bit of ground less soggy than the rest, there stood a ruined chapel.

Once more, the valiant little tailor told the men that the King sent to help him that he preferred to do his work by himself, and that they could wait out of sight. The Royal huntsmen were delighted to be given this order for, though they pretended to be very brave, they had already been several times to the marshes to hunt this particular boar, and he had chased them away and killed their dogs so often that they were all very much afraid of him. No wonder they were afraid! For this boar was a huge, heavy, tusker, with little red eyes and coal-black bristles. He could gallop at tremendous speed in spite of his weight, and he had such a furious temper that, once he was angry, he feared neither man nor dog.

So now, once more, the little tailor left his men and went quite alone on to the marsh, dodging about among the rushes and willows. It wasn't long before he heard tremendous gruntings, snortings, tramplings, and rootings. The huge boar seemed to get wind of the tailor almost as soon as the tailor heard him. The boar began to peer about, spied the tailor and then, instead of galloping off, the great furious beast rushed straight at him with flashing tusks and foaming jaws. Now what was the poor little tailor to do?

What he did do was to run for his life, but this wasn't much good, for the boar could gallop faster than the tailor could run, and this time there were no big trees for him to climb or hide behind, only little thin willows that would have bent even with his light weight. Then, just as the boar was so close that it seemed to the poor little man as if he could feel its hot breath on his legs, the tailor suddenly remembered the ruined chapel. With fresh hope in his heart he managed to put on an extra spurt of speed, saw it before him, saw that luckily the door was open, and dashed in. Close behind him and into the chapel thundered the boar, but, just as it had nearly reached him, the tailor sprang nimbly up on to a window-ledge, and then jumped out of the window. The boar was much too heavy to jump on to the window-ledge and far too big to get through the narrow window, and almost too big to turn round inside the chapel. Running round outside the chapel, while the boar blundered about

246

inside, the nimble little tailor was just in time to reach the door again and to bang it shut so that the boar was caught.

As soon as he had got his breath again, and when his heart had stopped pounding because of the dreadful fright he had had, the little tailor wiped his face, tidied his hair and then strolled calmly back to the Royal huntsmen, told them that he had the boar shut up in the chapel and that it would be quite safe for them to come and see. Great was their astonishment when, looking cautiously through the window, they actually saw that the dreadful old beast was a prisoner.

So now, when they had all got back to the castle, the King could think of no more excuses, and the wedding was solemnized with great splendour.

And that is how it came about that a valiant little tailor not only got a Princess as his wife, but also a kingdom — or at any rate half of one.

I went to the wedding. My bonnet was made of butter, but the sun melted it. My dress was made of spider's web but a thorn tore it. My slippers were made of glass but I slipped on some stones and they broke.